"Grac...

Cooper strode with caution toward the person.

Grace jolted to her feet and spun to face him. Blood covered her face and the front of her T-shirt.

"Cooper!" She stumbled to him and threw her arms around his neck, burying her face in his chest. Her tears soaked his shirt.

"I've got you."

"Cooper, please be careful." Her words were muffled.

"I'm more worried about you." He cupped her face, wiping away the remaining blood.

When she opened her eyes, the agony was impossible to miss. "The rope. I was driving your truck. The killer is after you."

He scrambled to make sense of her broken statements. "I'll be careful. I promise. Now, let's get you medical attention." He helped her walk through the woods, piecing together the meaning of her words. The crosshairs centered on him. But why?

His thoughts bounced from Gracie, and what had happened to her, to the target that, according to her, appeared to be on him. Had he messed up, and the killer discovered the reason he started bull riding again?

Award-winning, bestselling author **Sami A. Abrams** grew up hating to read. It wasn't until her thirties that she found authors who captured her attention. Most evenings, you can find her engrossed in a romantic suspense novel. She lives in Northern California but will always be a Kansas girl at heart. She has a love of sports, family and travel. However, writing her next story in a cabin at Lake Tahoe tops her list.

Books by Sami A. Abrams

Love Inspired Suspense

Tracking the Missing

Stone Creek Ranch

Christmas Rodeo Killer

Deputies of Anderson County

Buried Cold Case Secrets
Twin Murder Mix-Up
Detecting Secrets
Killer Christmas Evidence
Witness Escape

Visit the Author Profile page at LoveInspired.com.

CHRISTMAS RODEO KILLER

SAMI A. ABRAMS

LOVE INSPIRED SUSPENSE
INSPIRATIONAL ROMANCE

LOVE INSPIRED® SUSPENSE
INSPIRATIONAL ROMANCE

ISBN-13: 978-1-335-90635-9

Christmas Rodeo Killer

Copyright © 2025 by Sherryl Abramson

Love Inspired
22 Adelaide St. West, 41st Floor
Toronto, Ontario M5H 4E3, Canada
www.LoveInspired.com

Printed in U.S.A.

Recycling programs
for this product may
not exist in your area.

Casting all your care upon him; for he careth for you.
—*1 Peter* 5:7

This book is dedicated to my friend,
author Deborah Clack. Thank you for the fun-filled
phone calls and all the special things you've done
for me. I will never forget the first time we met.
The memory always makes me smile.

ONE

Private investigator and GracePoint Security owner Grace Harrison burrowed deep into the fleece lining of her jacket collar to ward off the cool night air. She left the rodeo arena lights and hubbub of the crowd and aimed herself toward the commotion at the far end of the parking lot. Easing her way toward bull rider Drake Bateman's camper-trailer where a small contingent of lookie-loos gaped at the unconscious cowboy, she spotted her childhood friend, Sheriff Isabelle "Izzie" Sinclair. The woman had her hands resting on her utility belt with her back to Grace, observing the paramedics from several feet away.

Grace slipped as close as possible without bringing attention to herself and studied the motionless body of the cowboy. She strained to hear any tidbit of information that might help her find solid evidence of murder to take to the county rodeo director Donovan Keats, the man who'd hired her to work undercover to investigate the deaths of four cowboys.

The four questionable deaths out of hundreds of bull riders over ten months during countless regional rodeos in or near Marshall County brought Grace full circle to the last place on earth she ever wanted to return—Rollins, Texas. But she shoved the anxiety aside and focused on discovering the truth. The four bull riders deserved justice if, in fact, their deaths had been at the hands of another.

As she stood at the edge of the small crowd, her nerves stretched tighter than a well-strung guitar. Working her third rodeo since Keats had approached her, Grace hadn't discovered a single clue contradicting the reports tied to the four cowboys' deaths, let alone who could have committed each crime. The authorities hadn't labeled the deaths as homicides but as accidents. And that theory smelled worse than a pile of horse manure. After reviewing the news articles and her company's deep dive into the public reports, she had little doubt that the bull riders from her region of Texas had a target on their backs. But why? And had the man lying on the gurney become the next victim?

Grace maneuvered closer and scanned the inside of the camper through the open door. Papers scattered the floor, and a small one-foot Christmas tree sat on the tiny kitchen table. No blood, but then again, from her quick assessment of Bateman, he didn't appear to have a gash on his head. The hurried glance into the man's temporary home revealed nothing obvious, but she'd mark a more thorough search on her to-do list for later. She had to be careful and not blow her cover. Not wanting to risk attracting attention, she tucked into the shadows, moving within earshot of the medical commotion.

A deputy pulled the sheriff aside. "There's a half-empty water bottle on the table and papers on the floor like he knocked them off when he collapsed."

"Evidence of head trauma?" Izzie shifted and crossed her arms.

The deputy shook his head. "No blood on the table or the floor." The man gestured to the paramedics. "And according to them, no lump or cut either."

Same assessment that Grace had made. Not wanting to miss additional information, she continued to stay close but out of sight.

"Let's keep this to ourselves. I don't want to cause a stir."

"You've got it, Sheriff. I let the rodeo director know that Bateman fell. It's close to the truth until we have a better grip on what happened."

"Thank you, Phil."

Grace ducked her head and wove between those watching, following Izzie as she strode toward the medics.

The sheriff informed the medical duo of the news that her deputy, Phil, would circulate around the rodeo. She requested the pair maintain silence beyond that and keep a low profile.

The female paramedic met Izzie's gaze. "Yes, ma'am. We won't say a word or announce our departure with lights or sirens." The woman's partner nodded in agreement.

Grace inched forward as the medics wheeled Drake to the waiting ambulance, not wanting to miss a single piece of information. A few minutes later, they whisked Bateman away from the parking lot beyond the rodeo arena without a fuss, heeding the sheriff's request.

The small crowd that had formed dispersed from the cowboy's camper-trailer, where his girlfriend, Macey Webster, had found him not more than twenty-five minutes ago.

From what she'd overheard earlier as the paramedics evaluated Drake's condition, Grace knew the cowboy had fallen unconscious due to unknown causes and became unresponsive. There had been no hit to the head, not contradicting local law enforcement's story of him falling. Grace texted Donovan Keats, the director of the rodeo and the man who hired her, confirming he received a message that Bateman had fallen. She'd wait to fill him in further until she had a better grasp of what had happened. But her brain flipped the information end to end, then sideways. Why the twisting of the truth? Why not just admit they didn't know the cause?

Grace moved along the shadowy perimeter away from the incident. Her presence at the rodeo was to work as a bullfighter. The story Keats spread that he'd requested her to fill in at the last minute for a man who'd been injured gave her presence believability. Doing a favor for a friend—that's why she was bullfighting again.

The phone in her pocket vibrated against her leg. Once far enough from the scene, she slipped behind a truck, glanced at the caller ID, and answered, "What did you find out?" After three rodeos, she prayed for the smallest morsel of information to point them in a solid direction. With the holiday rodeo the last until the start of next season, time had all but run out on finding evidence of a killer.

Her employee and second-in-command of her business, Cameron Winters, wasted no time. "Keats is right. The deaths are suspicious. You know how they say that nothing is—"

"Random. I take it you found a pattern."

"Yes and no. I've looked into other areas of Texas. There are no reported deaths of bull riders except for one, and he died of cancer. There's no distinct pattern. The months over the last year in which the deaths happened have varied, but they occur only in this area. And only during the current rodeo season for this region."

"And what about this rodeo? Marshall County Christmas Showdown is not exactly during prime season." Could they be fishing in an empty pond? Her gut said no, especially with Bateman's collapse.

"No, it's not, but it *is* an annual event."

"True. Back to our analysis. Each rider has a different cause of death, but all of those could have been a setup." Grace had studied the documents before accepting the investigation Keats had begged her to take. One of the reasons she'd agreed to the odd request.

"I don't understand why Sheriff Sinclair hasn't investigated these deaths." She could visualize Cameron running his fingers through his hair and leaving it standing on end.

"I don't know. Isabelle is an amazing law enforcement officer. I knew her growing up. Not examining these deaths isn't like her." She'd spent her childhood and teen years with Izzie Sinclair. More specifically, the woman's brother, Cooper. Grace and Cooper had been best friends. They'd known each other's secrets and dreams—well, most of them—until she'd blown it. A night she'd never forget for many reasons. The main one—a secret that no one from her hometown knew. And never would. She shook off the wayward thought. "It doesn't make sense. Granted, Marshall County is expansive, but all the deaths have happened here or in the next counties over. People talk. Why hasn't anyone said anything?"

"Whatever the reason, be careful, boss. I'm

going with the assumption that we have a killer on the loose, and by my calculations, he has another target in his sights as we speak. The guy will be acting soon."

She leaned forward and squinted in the direction of Bateman's camper. "Maybe he already has." Grace filled him in on the recent happenings.

"Could be. Do you want me to put someone on Bateman?"

"Qualifiers are in an hour. Drake won't be riding this rodeo, so I won't have eyes on him." She chewed on her thumbnail. "Get Laura down here. I don't want it to be obvious that we are protecting Bateman. Tell her to blend in at the hospital."

"You got it." Cameron grew silent.

Experience told her the man was sending out the job assignment, so she waited. A slow crunch of gravel sent a chill up her neck, and the icy fingers continued onto her scalp. Phone to her ear, she crouched low and slipped down the aisle of cars and trucks. She hid behind a huge tire and scanned under the vehicles. A pair of boots walked in a tight circle a mere twenty feet away. She froze in place.

"Are you okay, Grace?"

"Someone's here," she whispered.

"Do you need backup?" Cameron lowered his voice.

Did she? If she had her employee call for assistance, she'd blow her cover. No. She'd wait. "Hold."

Step by slow step, the thump of footfalls came closer. She held her breath and balanced on the balls of her feet, ready to spring into action if the need arose. A few moments later, the person moved away.

She released a lungful of air. "He's gone."

"Do you think someone figured out why you're really there?"

She rested the back of her head on the tire. Had she done anything to alert the killer? "I don't see how. I've been careful, and my story is solid." No one had questioned her appearance after all these years. Only hugs and *welcome back*s.

"I trust you. Don't hesitate to call if things go wonky. I can't blend in with the rodeo scene, but I'll have your six." The man might be a Texan, but he was as city as they came.

"I know, Cameron. And thank you. I'll be fine. Let me know when Laura is in place and what she discovers. Until then, I have to get ready for my bullfighter gig." She ended the call. If there was a killer out there targeting bull riders, what better place to be than in the arena with them?

As she strode to the barn, her mind spun to the Bateman situation. Had the killer struck again? Or had the man had a freak accident? The unknown person who'd walked away moments ago bothered her. What was he looking for? Had she messed up and exposed her reason for working the rodeo, placing a target on her back?

* * *

The all-too-familiar mix of hay, dust and manure tickled FBI agent Cooper Sinclair's nose. He snatched his cowboy hat from his head and crouched behind a stack of bedding straw. The position made his leg twinge, reminding him why he'd come home to Stone Creek Ranch in his hometown of Rollins, Texas, on a medical leave of absence four months ago. The bullet wound had healed, but he continued to experience aches if he shifted or stood in certain ways. Physical therapy had become a daily habit to regain muscle strength. In the beginning, some days had felt like a losing battle. Not to mention the psychological toll of taking the life of another human being, even if it had been self-defense.

He rubbed the sore muscles aggravated by being back on a bull again. He thought he'd left the bull-riding world behind when he joined the FBI. But no. Jared Parker, his special agent in charge, had to pull him into an undercover assignment. It beat riding a desk. Maybe. Probably not.

The heaters in the barn chased away the December chill but did little to warm the building to a cozy temperature. Cooper slowed his breathing and concentrated on the men around the corner.

"I told you not to make it obvious."

"Like these cowboys are smart enough to put it together."

"Just make sure you don't bring attention to yourself."

"Quit worrying, Billy."

Boots clomped on the packed dirt and faded into the background.

Cooper stood. His leather riding chaps heavy on his legs, he scanned the area inside the rodeo barn. Strings of multicolored Christmas lights looped from stall to stall. An oddity for sure. The Marshall County Christmas Showdown was a staple in the community, but the festive decor didn't mesh with the harsh reality of rodeo life.

The conversation he'd heard looped nonstop in his head. Billy? He mentally ran all the known names attached to the rodeo. Nope. He didn't know a Billy, but this was his first rodeo since he left for the FBI academy. The conversation was nondescript but had the possibility of leading him to the person responsible for the deaths of four bull riders over the past ten months. Deaths that people had accepted as accidents. Everyone except the sheriff, aka his sister Izzie.

His phone vibrated in his pocket. Maintaining his position in the shadows, he slid out the device and checked the text message. His buddy Luka's name popped up.

Luka: Schedule change. You're in the sixth slot riding Vortex. Bateman is out. Turbo pulled due to vet.

Great. Cooper had drawn the inexperienced bull Turbo that morning. The big lug was known for quickness, but his movements were predictable. However, they'd changed it up and given him Bateman's ride, Vortex. What had his sister Payton, the rodeo's veterinarian, discovered that made her sideline Turbo? His first rodeo in years. He did not need Vortex.

Cooper: What happened to Bateman?

Luka: IDK. Fell and hit his head or something. Get down here and gear up.

Cooper: On my way.

Not for the first time, Cooper wondered if he'd lost his mind agreeing to ride again. His eight-year-old daughter, Lexi, deserved a whole parent, not one broken into pieces on the arena ground. *Dramatic much?* He rolled his eyes at his ridiculous self and focused on the upcoming job. Get on the back of a bull. Ride for eight seconds. Jump off. Survive. Yeah, easier said than done. He thanked God for his recent physical therapy sessions and fitness routine.

He slapped his cowboy hat against his leg, placed it on his head and trudged to the staging area where he'd left his gear. His spurs rattled with each step. He used to love the excitement, but now, he dreaded it. He had no idea how Luka and Chris Reyes continued to ride. Sure, he missed the rodeo itself, but in his mind, he was too old for bull riding. Leave that to the younger men. He'd experienced it. Won some. Lost some. In the end, he'd walked away satisfied, with no regrets and no life-altering injuries. Why on earth had he allowed Parker to talk him into coming back? He shook his head and plodded on.

"There you are." Luka shoved Cooper's gloves and bull rope at him.

"Thanks for getting my stuff." He'd left it on his brother Daniel's footlocker. Having Daniel out there bullfighting gave Cooper a sense of calm in an otherwise heart-pounding situation.

Luka waved a hand. "No big deal."

"What did Payton say happened to Turbo?" He'd find his veterinarian sister later and ask her directly, but he was curious what Luka had heard.

"The bull had a cut on his leg, so she pulled him."

"Too bad." Call him suspicious, but Cooper wondered if the injury was an accident or intentional. Of course, he had thought the same thing about Bateman's fall. Could someone have caused the man to hit his head? He agreed with his sister's skepticism about the four deaths during the season but hadn't found proof as of yet.

"Yeah, I know you studied that bull and knew

every move. But it's not like you didn't study Vortex too."

Cooper lifted his hat and scratched his head. "Vortex is brutal. He's experienced, and the way he switches directions…" He blew out a long breath and replaced his hat. *Lord, help me survive this insanity. I just want a peaceful life with my daughter.*

"You mean the top-of-the-heap bull rider can't handle a challenge." Luka threw his head back and laughed.

"Not the top anymore. I gave it up, or did you forget that part? For now, I'm back to help promote the Christmas Showdown. We'll see about next season. Besides, I need a break from the FBI." Cooper hadn't lied. The case that had gone bad had both mental and physical ramifications.

Luka slapped him on the back. "Whatever the reason, I, for one, am glad to have you back. I've missed you on the circuit. These new kids are a bit too cocky for their own good."

"I've enjoyed hanging out. Kind of like old times." Cooper had missed the camaraderie. The groups that competed together often formed their own family of sorts.

Luka threw his arm around Cooper's shoulder. "You can say that again, brother. The dynamic duo is back in action."

Yeah, he'd missed his crazy friend more than

he cared to admit. They'd had some good times in the past.

Cooper waited near the chute for his turn and prepped the equipment for his ride.

"Oh, too bad." The announcer's voice boomed through the arena. "Everyone, give it up for Combs. Next up, our returning hometown hero, Cooper Sinclair. Due to a change in the schedule, Drake Bateman is a scratch, and Cooper Sinclair will be riding Vortex."

A hushed murmur fell over the crowd.

He understood. The idea of getting on Vortex sent icy fingers crawling up his spine. At least his daughter, Lexi, had stayed with his mom at the ranch. The last thing he wanted was for his eight-year-old to see his broken body sprawled on the arena ground. He shook off the morbid thought and got his head on straight.

Eight seconds. That's all he had to do. Cooper closed his eyes and visualized the ride. The quick whip turns would be difficult, but he'd be fine as long as he stayed centered. He inhaled and released the air in a long stream.

He glanced at Luka. "Let's do this."

Luka's smile engulfed his face. "Come on, man, show these young'uns how it's done."

The Black Angus bull slammed against the chute, rattling the metal. Huffs filled the small space. Again, why had Cooper agreed to this? He sent up a prayer for safety in his first official go. Gripping the top of the chute, he toed his boot between the slats and hoisted himself onto the gate. He glanced into the arena and spotted two bullfighters midway in the ring. He knew his brother Daniel was one of them. The other, with a cowboy hat covering his face—he wasn't sure about. He'd heard Ronnie pulled out due to an injury. Not that it mattered who had taken the man's place. If Cooper got in trouble, his younger brother would get him out of it. They'd played this game too many times in the past. Cooper rode. Daniel played catch. A part of him wished for Gracie. She and Daniel had made an unstoppable team. But the past was the past. Or so he kept telling himself. Her betrayal had dug a deep gouge in his heart. Over time and with the help of his deceased wife, the wound had healed—mostly. He had to admit he missed the best friend from his youth.

"Let's get you on." The cowboy helping at the chute gestured toward Vortex.

Cooper shook off his wayward thoughts. No time for could've, would've, should've. He double-checked his protective vest and slid his hands into his leather gloves. "Coming in."

He took three breaths and focused on the immediate task. After adjusting his vest, he swung his leg over the rail and lowered himself onto Vortex's back. The bull lurched inside the enclosure. Cooper shot up, narrowly missing his leg getting smashed against the metal rails. He let the animal settle and lowered himself once again. *Easy, big fella. I don't like this any more than you do.*

The helper attached the bull strap around Vortex's flank, and Cooper wrapped the bull rope that looped the animal's chest around his hand in his normal pre-ride rhythmic fashion. Wrap, tug, adjust, repeat. Tight enough not to slip but not so much that he couldn't get his hand out. He shifted and centered his weight. Eight seconds. He could do this. And with this bull's experience, Vortex would rack up points, and Cooper would move on to the next round. Assuming he lasted the full ride. No. He would last. He had to.

"You've got this, Coop." Luka held out Cooper's mouthpiece.

"Thanks." He opened his mouth, and his friend slid the plastic over his teeth.

"Ready?"

Cooper secured his hat with his free hand, wondering what had possessed him not to wear the helmet. He gave a quick nod.

The metal door to the chute swung open. Cooper lifted his right arm. Vortex shot out and twisted to his right, then to the left. Cooper's body whipped forward and back. He struggled to keep his center of balance. The bull was at the top of his game, and Cooper wasn't. He tightened his core, relied on his extensive experience and hung on.

The roar of the crowd vanished. His attention—

solely on the beast trying to buck him off. The thud of hooves echoed in his ear. Snot from the bull's nostrils slung into the air. Cooper willed the buzzer to go off. If he clenched his teeth any harder, he'd break a molar. The strap around the bull attached to his hand slipped. He clutched the rope firmer.

The buzzer sounded, and cheers went up around the arena. He'd made it.

Cooper shifted to dismount. Before he released his hand, the strap gave way. Off balance, with Vortex continuing to twist and turn, Cooper flew off the bull's back and landed with a thud. Air whooshed from his lungs, and bright lights shot like fireworks behind his eyes.

"Coop, right!" Daniel's words registered in his muddled mind.

He tucked and rolled in the direction his brother commanded, but his reaction time was a tad too late. Vortex's hoof caught the edge of his shoulder and scraped down his protective vest. Pain sliced through his side. He curled in on himself, praying the bull didn't make contact with his head. He had a daughter to raise, and he couldn't do that dead.

Grace's stomach threatened to empty as her childhood best friend, Cooper, lay on the ground in a fetal position. The two-thousand-pound bull lowered his head, ready to charge. She shook off the shock and ran toward the man and animal, determined to do her job as a bullfighter.

"Grace, get the bull!" Her rodeo partner, Daniel, headed toward his brother.

Vortex moved in for another attack. She veered off and placed herself between Cooper and the massive animal. A shout and a quick wave of her hands had the bull changing direction. She side-stepped Vortex's attempt to gore her and moved toward the protective barrel in the middle of the arena, encouraging the hunk of meat to follow her as she raced away from the men. With Vortex angling away from Cooper, she concentrated on her goal. Get the bull out of the arena and into the holding area. Two cowboys on horseback came riding to her aid and released the flank strap. Vortex's attitude changed. He no longer wanted to take his frustrations out on her. The animal trotted toward the fence. Grace moved out of the way and let the heroes on horseback guide Vortex to the exit.

The black beast moved through the gate, and another cowboy slammed it closed.

She wiped the sweat from her forehead and sprinted to the other side of the arena. Her cleats slid through the dirt. On her knees beside Cooper, she inspected him head to toe. "How is he?"

"He's woozy, and from the way Vortex's hoof caught him, he'll have some massive bruising if not a break." Daniel waved for the paramedics to join them.

"Gracie?" Cooper whispered.

She jerked her attention to the man who had stolen her heart years ago, but she'd never admit that to him or anyone else. "I'm right here."

"What…doing?" His words slurred.

"Came back for old times bullfighting with Daniel." Grace slipped her hand into his and squeezed.

He returned the pressure. "Thanks." He blinked several times.

She moved aside, allowing the medics space to treat him, but didn't release his hand.

Luka hurried in. The bull rope used on Vortex hung from his fingers. "Is he okay?"

"I'll be fine. Just a little banged-up." Cooper's words had cleared since she'd arrived at his side moments ago.

"Yeah, he's hardheaded and stubborn." Daniel smiled, albeit a little forced, and tweaked the toe of Cooper's boot.

"Back at ya, brother."

Several minutes later, the medic closest to her announced, "We're ready to transport."

Grace stood and collected Cooper's equipment. She motioned for Luka to give her the rope. "I'll take that and store his stuff for him."

Luka hesitated but didn't argue. "I'm done with my ride. I'm heading to the hospital with him."

"I'll be there as soon as we finish here." Daniel patted Cooper on the leg. "Don't annoy the doctors."

Cooper groaned. "I hate hospitals."

"I know." Daniel laughed at Cooper's expression.

There was a story there. Grace knew it, but she refused to ask. She hadn't seen Cooper in years. Her guilt and shame had forced her to stay away, along with the fear that surrounded her life in Rollins, Texas.

Bull rope over her shoulder, she headed to her footlocker inside the barn to store Cooper's gear while Daniel dealt with his brother. The announcer would give everyone a moment to recover from the incident before calling the next bull rider to the chutes. And she'd readily admit she required a few minutes to stuff her heart back in her chest. She hadn't expected to come face-to-face with the only man she'd ever loved.

The clank of spurs and footfalls of cowboy boots blended with the chatter among those working or participating in the rodeo. Grace placed Cooper's equipment into the metal box for safekeeping until he recovered from his injuries. The end of his bull rope grabbed her attention. She lifted the braided material. What in the world? With her focus on Cooper, she'd missed it. A clean slice partway into the nylon. Someone had severed a section of his rope. It hadn't snapped in two but had separated enough for him to lose his balance. She'd seen him prepare to jump off when he'd fallen instead. If she hadn't examined the cut, she would've assumed his tumble was an accident.

"Yo, Grace, time to go," Daniel called from the entrance to the arena.

"Coming." She stuffed the evidence in her trunk and secured the latch. Too many accidents had happened to the bull riders recently, and that's why she was there—to keep an eye on things. However, none of the deaths occurred during the rodeos. Why the change? Assuming there was one. And why would anyone want to hurt Cooper? Had his return to his previous profession triggered someone? She brushed off the questions swirling in her mind and jogged to Daniel's side.

"Let's do this." The man smiled. He still loved bullfighting. Her? Not as much as she used to, but since the rodeo director hired her to protect his bull riders and investigate the odd happenings, inside the inner circle was the best place to be.

"Are you heading to the hospital later?" Grace closed the gate behind her, and the pair's cleats kicked up dirt as they jogged to their spots, ready for the next rider.

"That's my plan. By the time we're done working, the doc should've finished with him." Daniel, in his county rodeo shirt, stuck one thumb under his red suspenders and swung the colorful scarves attached to his oversized long shorts in a circle with his other hand like a flapper girl swinging her beads. He smiled. "Ready?"

"You're a goof." She rolled her eyes and tried to hide her smile. "Let's do this."

Yup, she'd missed the Sinclair siblings. One of the few good memories of her hometown.

Forty-five minutes later, after the last bull rider exited the arena, Daniel slapped her on the back in a brotherly fashion. "That was fun. I'm glad you're back. I don't mind working with Ronnie—he's a good guy. But he and I don't have the same working chemistry as we do."

Sweaty, dirty, and tired, she nodded. "We've had our fair share of jobs together. Guess that's why we can anticipate each other's movements." Even after years of not working side by side, it hadn't taken long for her and Daniel to find their rhythm. Muscle memory was a thing.

"Very true." Daniel strolled with her from the holding area to the parking lot. He grabbed his duffel from the back seat of his truck, lowered the tailgate and peeled off the outer layer of clothes, leaving him in gym shorts and a T-shirt. His cleats came off next, replaced by tennis shoes. "This will do until I check on Coop."

She'd parked herself next to him on the back of his truck and matched his actions. A hot bath sounded fantastic, but she'd head to the barn bathrooms, shower and change into her jeans and boots since she still had work to do. Many of the bull riders hung out behind the scenes after the event. She intended to make herself part of the background and hope for a clue to what really happened to the four bull riders.

She jumped down and scooped up the outer clothes she'd shed. "I plan to stick around here for a bit. But I'll head to the hospital to see how Cooper is doing in a little while. Could you send me a text on his condition?"

"Will do." Daniel slammed the tailgate closed. "Funny thing. I've never known him to fall off like that. Bucked off? Sure. But he lost his balance or something. I suppose anything could happen, especially with his leg injury, but the way he went down makes no sense. Maybe he's just out of practice."

Her movements halted. "What happened to Cooper's leg?"

"Shot during his last case. The whole situation was ugly." Daniel's gaze connected with hers. "By the look on your face, I guess you didn't know that."

"No. But I haven't been around in a long time." Try years.

"True." He shrugged. "Anyway, I'll keep you posted. I'm sure he'd like you to come visit."

She doubted that. Not the way she'd ghosted him after their one night together. A night that had changed everything. "I'll catch you later." She waved and strolled to the barn. Daniel's observation spun in her head. And where did the frayed end of Cooper's bull rope fit in?

After a quick shower, she said hi to the cowboys and pretended to have a reason for hanging around. An hour later, she had nothing to work with, so Grace left the rodeo grounds and drove to the hospital. Daniel's earlier text had informed her that Cooper had somehow managed to avoid a concussion but had a bruised shoulder and ribs along with several lacerations on his back and face. And one massive headache.

Once she parked her SUV near the entrance of the Marshall County General Hospital, Grace strode inside.

Swoops of red-and-gold garland hung in loops on the front of the hospital reception desk. Christmas lights framed the countertop, and "Away in a Manger" played softly in the background.

Grace hadn't enjoyed Christmas as a child. Not until she spent the majority of her teenage years with the Sinclairs. Miss Hannah never disappointed. Cookies, music, decorations. But Grace's favorite—the ten-foot-tall tree in the ranch house living room where Mrs. Sinclair displayed her children's homemade ornaments among the fancier ones. Grace's parents' tree had always been elegant and designer-worthy. No special handmade ornaments in sight. Not that her mother had encouraged her to make any either. One of the many childhood memories she'd never experienced.

Her boots clomped on the hospital tile as she walked toward room 106. The idea of speaking with Cooper after nine years terrified and excited her. Growing up, he'd been her best friend. Always there when she needed a shoulder to lean on. They'd dabbled with a relationship back then, but their one night during college had ruined everything. And that had been all her fault. Her stupid desperation to be loved had fractured any possible future together.

The door to the room was open a crack. Grace hesitated, unsure how he'd react to her presence. But she wasn't a timid girl anymore. Taking a deep breath, she shoved aside her insecurities and knocked. "Cooper?"

"Come in." His gravelly voice made her smile. Oh, how she missed the gruff sound.

She eased the door open. "Hi."

His gaze connected with hers, and he gaped at her.

Ignoring his shock, she waltzed in. "Sorry, it took me a while to get here. Daniel kept me up to date with text messages." She moved next to him, where he lay with the head of the bed raised to a forty-five-degree angle. The black-and-blue mark on his cheek looked painful. As did the cuts. From what Daniel had told her, those were nothing compared to the bruises on his back and torso.

"What are you doing here?" The words weren't cruel, but they stabbed her heart just the same.

She dipped her chin. Yeah, she deserved that. "I watched Vortex almost stomp on you. Where else would I be?"

"Sorry. That didn't come out right. I'm just surprised to see you."

"I understand." And she did. After their one night together, they'd gone back to their lives. Her at college, and him at the FBI academy. She hadn't seen or talked to him since—on purpose. Her reason? Guilt, plain and simple.

"I didn't know you decided to bullfight again. According to Izzie, you're a successful businesswoman." He fidgeted with the blanket draped over his lap.

"The rodeo's a temporary gig. And yes, my security business is doing very well. I've expanded to add personal security to my list of services. I employ fifteen people now."

He whistled through his teeth. "You *are* doing well."

She cocked her head. "And why are you back on the bulls again? I thought you gave that up for the FBI, and according to your sister, when I ran into her six years ago, you're happily married with a daughter."

"Word gets around, doesn't it?" He exhaled. "I'm on a…let's call it a break from my job. I had an incident and took medical leave. But my mind still needs time to heal." His hand massaged his thigh. Most likely a subconscious action. "My wife, Kaitlyn, passed away four years ago. So now I'm sporting the title of single dad."

"I'm so sorry. I had no idea." That had to be rough on him. She knew what it was like to lose the love of your life because she'd lost Cooper nine years ago. A bit different, but yet, the same in many ways.

"It's okay. My daughter, Lexi, and I are doing well. Minus the work incident." His gaze drifted to the far wall. She let the quiet linger. He blinked and refocused on her. "I'm guessing you haven't visited Rollins in a while."

She shook her head. Why would she come back to the horrors of her hometown? "I live in Lackard and haven't been back since before the last time I saw you."

"Long time to be away from home."

"Not when my parents are here." She avoided them like a charging bull.

Realization flickered in his eyes. "I take it dear old daddy hasn't changed?"

"Nope." Since she'd left town, she'd shoved away the memories of her father's abuse and her mother's disregard of his actions. Then again, had her mom known the extent of his hatred for her daughter? "Let's change topics."

Cooper clamped his mouth shut and nodded. A few moments later, he met her gaze. "Thank you for helping me tonight. Daniel said he gave you the bull while he came to my aid."

She waved off his kindness. "You're welcome, but you know that's what we do."

"I know, but I would've felt horrible if you'd gotten hurt." His brow scrunched.

"What is it?" She moved closer to his side but refused to reach for his hand.

"I can't fathom how things went bad so quickly. I hit the eight seconds and shifted to jump off." He stared at the cream-colored wall across from him as if the answer would appear.

"Cooper?"

"My bull rope gave way, and I slid."

"How in the world would that happen?" She possessed the proof his bull rope had been cut, but she wanted his thoughts without leading him. Her short-lived career as an army intelligence officer demanded it.

"Not a clue. It shouldn't have." His eyes drooped closed and then popped open. "Sorry. They gave me pain meds. I'm drifting on you."

"Completely understandable. I'll let you get some rest. We'll talk more later." She fought the urge to lean down and kiss his forehead. "Good night, Cooper."

"'Night, Gracie." His barely-above-a-whisper words hit her chest dead center.

No one had ever called her Gracie except him. When his breathing evened out, she tore her gaze from his battered face and slipped into the hall, pondering what to do next. She might be excellent at private investigations and protection with her intelligence background, but law enforcement wasn't in her wheelhouse. She scoped out the first floor of the hospital and found an out-of-the-way place to sit with a view of his door.

Meandering her way to the chairs, she let her mind swirl with the day's events. The frayed end of the bull rope and Cooper's incident added up to something fishy going on. Had the killer targeted Cooper? And what about Bateman?

She dropped onto the seat and pulled her phone from her pocket. She shot off a text message to Cameron and Laura and received an update on Bateman.

Laura: Safe, but no change.

Grace leaned back in the chair and got comfortable. Tomorrow, she'd figure out her next step. Tonight, she'd make sure no one hurt Cooper while he slept.

TWO

The bruises on Cooper's torso and shoulder ached, but he'd thanked God over and over last night that Vortex hadn't made a direct hit with his hooves. The recliner and extra pillow he'd commandeered at his mother's house on Stone Creek Ranch did little to alleviate the soreness from the bull-riding incident—a failed dismount that continued to puzzle him.

The latest rendition of "O Come, All Ye Faithful" filtered in from the kitchen where his mom and his daughter, Lexi, baked cookies and sang Christmas carols together. He stared at the giant Christmas tree in the corner of the living room, searching the twinkling lights for the answer to the odd happenings.

God, what am I missing?

He pinched the bridge of his nose. What had happened to cause his bull rope to give way? He'd been out of practice, sure. But that had no effect on his attempted and failed dismount. He'd shifted his weight, but the rope hadn't held firm.

"You think any harder, and your brain will explode."

Cooper glanced up and found his sister standing at the entrance to the living room in her sheriff's uniform with her arms crossed.

"Hey, Izzie." He motioned to the couch. "Have a seat."

She settled on the cushion next to his chair. "How's the ribs and shoulder?"

"It doesn't feel great, but I've had worse." Might as well be honest with the human lie detector staring at him.

His sister ran a practiced eye over his face and torso. "Are you going to be able to ride in the team roping with Daniel tonight?"

Wasn't that the question of the day? "I'll manage. I can't exactly do my job if I'm not with the rest of the cowboys. Besides, Daniel has a more demanding job as the heeler. All I have to do as the header is rope the steer's horns or neck." He chuckled, then grabbed his ribs and groaned.

Izzie shook her head and peeked over her shoulder, confirming they were alone. "Does anyone else know about your undercover assignment besides your supervisor, Special Agent Parker?"

"Only you and Jared. As you know, I'm here under the pretense of needing medical leave. However, he's dropped hints, and my team thinks I'm having second thoughts about going back to work. So no one on that front is aware. As for the rodeo community, they're curious about why I'm back. The word on the street is that I'm promoting the December rodeo. By the way, you've done a good job laying that groundwork for me." He chuckled. "The impression is that I plan to return to the circuit next season. I have no idea where that came from, but I'm going with it."

Izzie's shoulders drooped. "I'm sorry I brought you into the investigation. When I contacted Special Agent Parker, I didn't anticipate he'd have you undercover as a bull rider."

Cooper shrugged, careful not to aggravate his injuries. "What better way to discover what's going on?" He'd balked at riding again, but in the end, he and his boss decided it would be the best way to conduct the investigation.

"True. But still. I'm sorry I dragged you back into that world."

"It's in our blood. You know that. Besides, you agreed to barrel race again. We both are coming out of rodeo retirement." He gave a dramatic sigh.

Izzie laughed. "Never thought I'd race in competition now that I'm sheriff."

Cooper smiled. "I hear ya."

His sister leaned forward and rested her elbows on her knees. "So, what went wrong last night? I've seen you thrown before. And you know how to dismount away from a bull. Last night, you literally slid off. What's up with that?"

"I might have the answer to that question." A woman's voice interrupted their conversation.

Cooper jerked his head to the living room entrance, and Izzie shot to her feet.

"Sorry. I didn't mean to eavesdrop." Grace Harrison stood ten feet away, holding a bag.

She'd stopped by his hospital room last night, but he'd been doped up on pain meds and barely remembered their conversation. He drank her in like a man desperate for a glass of water. The woman was as gorgeous as ever. Her hair had grown longer, and her riotous blond curls draped over her shoulders. She had matured. Had a more confident look about her, but other than that, she appeared to be the same Grace he'd grown up with.

"Your mother let me in and told me to join you in here."

Izzie rushed to Grace's side and threw her arms around the woman. "It's good to see you. And thank you for saving my brother last night."

"It's all part of the job." Grace's gaze met his. "I'm happy to see you upright."

Memories of their night together and the subsequent disappearance from each other's lives jumbled his words. Unable to trust his voice, he nodded.

"Come, have a seat and tell us what you mean by you might have the answer." Izzie motioned to the couch. Both women sat.

Grace fiddled with the bag handle she held in a tight grip. "After the paramedics hauled you away, I gathered your equipment and put it in my footlocker. I noticed something strange with your bull rope." She extracted the braided cord and held up one end. "It's frayed."

"As if it had been cut." He finished Grace's thought. "I noticed it loosened during the ride. When I lifted to jump off, it gave way. That explains why I slipped."

Izzie narrowed her gaze. "You think someone tampered with it?"

He shrugged. "Could have." The fact Cooper obsessed about the condition of his equipment meant that sabotage made the most sense.

"So, is the killer targeting you?" Grace flipped the frayed end of the bull rope back and forth.

"Wait." Izzie shifted to face Grace. "What killer are you talking about?"

"Don't deny it. I heard you discussing Cooper being undercover before I walked in. And the only reason for that is the four bull riders who've died over the past ten months."

He narrowed his gaze. "How do you know about that?" No one in the circuit had put the pieces together since the deaths happened at different locations and by other means.

Grace's eyes drifted to the floor, and she twisted her mouth to the side. He hadn't forgotten her *I can't decide what to say* expression.

"Gracie?"

"Fine. Since you're both law enforcement and we're on the same side, I suppose it's okay to tell you." Her eyes met his. "Director Keats hired me as extra security for the rodeo and to investigate the *odd* occurrences. My focus is on the bull riders. He told me to snoop around—his words, not mine—and see if I can discover evidence of foul play to take to the police. Aka Izzie."

"*That's* why you're bullfighting." All the pieces fell into place—her return to Rollins and her sudden reappearance working for the county rodeo.

She nodded. "It's easier to blend in if I'm part of the working crew." Grace cocked her head to the side. "If I overheard correctly, same for you."

How much should he tell her? Considering his sister was the local law enforcement around these parts, he glanced at her for guidance. She shrugged. *Thanks a lot, Sis.*

"Yes. I was home recovering from an in-the-line-of-duty injury when Izzie approached my boss. He requested I go undercover as a bull rider. She and I—" he pointed to his sister "—agreed, since that seems to be the focus of the killer."

"Do you have proof that someone actually killed those cowboys?" Grace laid the rope in her lap.

Cooper cringed at the careless handling of evidence, but the rope had already been compromised, so he stayed quiet.

"In a manner of speaking." Izzie stepped into the conversation. "I've kept it contained and continued to investigate since the evidence isn't irrefutable one way or the other as to murder or accident. But it is questionable. The medical examiner confided in me that he suspected homicide, but he couldn't document his gut feelings. I figured if word got out that there was a possibility the deaths were intentional, the guy would move on, and we'd never catch him since it's the end of the season."

"What do you have, if you don't mind me asking?" Grace shifted to face Izzie.

"The autopsy reports show inconsistencies. Injuries covering other injuries. Habits that don't match the victim's normal day-to-day life. Things like that. But nothing that will hold up in court."

"Izzie had enough questions as to the cause of deaths that she convinced my boss. He assigned me to the case since I'm already here and technically hadn't returned from leave."

"So, you're fishing, just like me." Grace's statement hit the problem on the head.

Cooper winced at the truth of her words. "That's one way to put it."

"This is my third rodeo investigating for Director Keats. Let me work with you. I'm a good PI." Grace glanced at him and then at Izzie. "I have resources you can't justify the cost for."

He raised a brow. "Like?"

"For one, I already have a bodyguard on Drake Bateman. Nobody will know why she's there, and she knows how to blend in."

"That's Izzie's determination. I'm just here to do the grunt work." Cooper waggled his eyebrows at his sister.

Izzie stuck her tongue out at him. "As if." She addressed Grace. "I've heard about your business's reputation. It's top-notch. Since I'm on a fishing expedition, as you called it, I'll agree to bring you and your company in. As long as this stays under wraps."

"Thank you. It will make my job for Keats easier, and maybe we'll figure out who is killing these men."

"That's the goal."

Cooper rested his head against the recliner. For whatever reason, having another person in on the investigation eased his concerns a bit.

Lexi, his eight-year-old daughter, flitted into the room, her left hand fisted, and a glass of water in her right hand. "Grandma said not to complain and to take these." She produced three ibuprofen tablets on her palm.

"Grandma's a bit bossy." His heart exploded with love when Lexi laughed at his fake grumpy face. He accepted the medicine and popped it in his mouth. After drinking half the water, he placed the glass on the end table. "Thanks, princess."

His daughter kissed his cheek. "You're welcome, Daddy."

He motioned to Grace. "Lexi, I'd like you to meet…" How did he introduce the two? He paused a moment and went with the safe route. "My friend Grace."

Lexi skipped over to the couch and held out her hand. "It's nice to meet you, Miss Grace."

Grace shook his daughter's hand. "And you as well. You seem to take excellent care of your father."

"Someone has to. He'd lose everything if I didn't watch out for him." She turned her head and gave him a cheesy grin.

He grabbed his chest and feigned distress. "Lexi, I'm wounded."

"No, you're not. Silly daddy."

"You know, I grew up with your father, and he'd misplace his truck keys all the time," Grace whispered in a conspiratorial tone.

"He still does." His daughter and the woman who'd vanished from his life nine years ago laughed together.

Izzie's eyes shifted to the pair who enjoyed the teasing comments and back to him. Her eyes widened.

Uh-oh. Cooper never thought anyone would figure out his secret since Lexi was his female mini-me. But obviously, his sister had latched onto the truth. Or she thought she had. He shook his head to stave off the question.

His sister's eyes narrowed. Growing up, he'd been on the receiving end of her interrogations a few too many times. It was no wonder she excelled at her position as sheriff. He mouthed *later*.

Izzi rolled her eyes. But he knew she'd keep her questions and assumptions to herself—for now.

"I have to get back to Grandma." Lexi leveled her gaze at him. A tear shimmered in her eye. His daughter worried about him but played it off. "Feel better, Daddy. I love you."

"Love you too, princess." He never got tired of hearing those words from her. To think he almost missed the opportunity.

"I'll go help Mom and give you two time to catch up." Izzie steered Lexi out of the living room.

Grace shifted on the couch, fidgeting with the hem of her shirt.

"Gracie."

Her eyes popped up. "You're the only person ever to call me that."

"Grace was too stuffy for you. You've always been Gracie to me." The nickname had slipped out from the moment he'd seen her in the arena. Maybe he shouldn't keep calling her that. Old memories and all that. "Is it okay? Or would you rather not hear it?"

"It's fine. Just took me by surprise last night."

He nodded. Him too, if he were honest. "Gracie, I owe you an apology."

"What for?"

"That night we spent together nine years ago. I shouldn't have touched you."

Grace straightened. "Cooper Sinclair, I'm the one who owes *you* an apology. I took advantage of our friendship. I wanted to be loved so badly…" Her words trailed off.

"You deserved to be loved after everything your parents put you through." He sighed. "Can we agree that we both went about things the wrong way?"

"That sounds fair." Grace's mouth opened like she planned to say more but then chose not to.

He'd hoped she'd admit to what she had done after that night. It hurt that she continued to keep her secret. But then again, so did he. "So, tell me about your security company."

Her entire demeanor changed. The tension that lined her features disappeared. "After our… well, you know…our night together, I finished school and about a year later joined the army to escape life. My recruiting officer suggested I go into army intelligence. So, I signed up and never looked back. I excelled at my job but soon realized I didn't want to make the army my career." She shrugged. "I served my time and landed in

Lackard, Texas. I got my private investigator's license and opened my own business, GracePoint Security. It didn't take long before I expanded the services and hired more staff."

"How many do you have now? I think you told me, but last night is a bit fuzzy." The fact she lived in Lackard and they hadn't run into each other had shocked him. Then again it was a large city. But her success hadn't surprised him. He'd known if she could escape from her father's grip, she'd be unstoppable at anything she wanted to do.

"There are fifteen of us. I might add a few more in the future, but fifteen is perfect for right now."

"Sounds like you've done well for yourself." He was so proud of her for getting out from under her parents' toxic home.

"Becoming a well-respected business was always the goal." Grace checked her watch and then dug her keys out of her pocket. "Speaking of, I better get going. I have to meet with my employee Laura, who's shadowing Drake Bateman at the hospital."

"You think he's the next target." Cooper shifted to ease the pressure on his ribs.

She nodded. "I do. I hung around his trailer, trying to glean information. A couple of things piqued my interest, but I'm not ruling out other possibilities. Especially after your bull rope broke. I'm definitely curious about how that happened."

She placed a tentative hand on his arm. "Be careful. You could be this guy's next objective."

He clutched her fingers, unprepared for the resurfacing of emotions it triggered. "Thank you for coming and for saving me last night."

She smiled and pulled her hand away. "You're welcome."

Cooper pushed himself upright and waited for the aches to subside. "I'll see you out."

He walked beside her. Neither spoke—it was as if they both had tumbled into the past.

"Once I hear from Laura, I'll text you and Izzie with an update."

"I appreciate that." He retrieved her jacket from the coat tree, held it for her to slip on, then opened the door.

She stepped out into the December chill. "See you tonight."

"Later, Gracie." He shoved his hands in his pockets to ward off the cool temperatures and leaned against the doorjamb, waiting for her to get into her car and leave.

His conscience nagged at him that he hadn't fessed up to the truth he'd hidden from Grace and his family. He'd blame his brush with death last night, but the hurt from her betrayal all those years ago was the real culprit. And he'd compounded the problem by letting his family believe what they'd wanted instead of setting the record straight.

* * *

Guilt smothered Grace as she strode toward her SUV. Memories, good and bad, assaulted her. But seeing Cooper with Lexi pierced her heart. Her daughter would be about the same age as Lexi. She imagined for a moment what the little girl would look like. Would she have Cooper's black hair and green eyes, or blond hair and blue eyes like her? A tiny whimper escaped her lips. What had caused her to have been so cruel? Her parents held that honor. The backlash of not being the perfect daughter had overwhelmed her sense of right and wrong—that, along with fear.

The night she'd shared with Cooper had led to a pregnancy she'd never told anyone about. She'd given birth, signed the adoption papers and left, never looking back. She'd cheated Cooper out of the opportunity to be a father to *their* child.

Tears burned behind her eyes. Swallowing hard, she blinked back the waterworks. She rounded the car and came to an abrupt halt. A flat front tire grabbed her attention. Just great.

"Gracie, what's wrong?" Cooper's worried tone snapped her out of her pity party.

"My tire's flat." She retrieved her phone from her jacket and checked the time. "And I'm supposed to meet with Laura in twenty minutes."

"Hang on." He ducked inside and returned a moment later. "Take my truck. I'll catch a ride with either Izzie or Daniel."

"Are you sure?"

"Positive. Mine's the black F150."

She jogged to the front steps and collected his keys. "Thanks. I appreciate it. I'll come back out later and change the tire."

He waved her off. "Someone will take care of it and bring it to you."

"That's not necessary."

"But it'll happen." He quirked an eyebrow, daring her to continue the argument.

"Fine. You win." She jiggled the keys. "Thanks again." If she hadn't had to be in town soon, she would've simply changed the tire on her own.

Several minutes later, she drove past Cooper and waved goodbye. It had been a hot minute since she'd driven a truck that size, but she'd get the hang of it by the time she arrived in town— like riding a bike and all that. She snorted. A rather large bike.

Dust flew from under the tires as she drove down the long lane to the Stone Creek Ranch entrance. The pastures on both sides had dried and turned brown due to the season and dropping winter temperatures. But her mind pictured the green grass sprinkled with wildflowers she and Cooper used to ride through during the summers. She missed her time spent on the ranch during her teen years. A refuge from her life at home. Horses had become her sanity. She and Cooper would ride for hours until she could face the world again. She wiped the tear that had trickled down her cheek and pushed the speed dial for Laura. It rang, echoing through the cab from the speaker on her phone.

"Hey, boss. Aren't we meeting in about twenty minutes?"

"Hi, Laura. Yes, but you know me. I want an update before I get there so I can mull over the information." Grace gripped the steering wheel and exited the ranch, turning onto the county road. She glanced in the rearview mirror. A purple pillow and stuffed raccoon brought a sad smile to her face. Cooper would have his hands full in a few years with Lexi. The young girl with her father's eye and hair color was beautiful. Boys would trip all over themselves to date his daughter. Grace's eyes drifted to the road behind her and back in the direction of town.

"I figured you'd call before our meeting." Laura chuckled. "No change in Bateman's condition. He's still unconscious. However, I did hear the doctors discussing him."

"Hiding in plain sight again, I see." Grazing cows dotted the landscape to her right, and trees lined the other side of the road, forming the edge of the woods that stretched for miles. She adjusted the air vent and pointed the stream of warm air toward her. The cool December day made her thankful for the working heater.

"Nah, just doing my job." Laura's voice held a bit of pride.

Grace had won the prize the day she'd hired Laura. The woman had stealth down to an art form, and her defensive skills—unbelievable for her size. Laura constantly joked she was fun-size. The description fit her perfectly at five foot one and a bundle of energy.

Grace's gaze latched onto a dark SUV in the rearview mirror, approaching her at an impressive speed. The manic driver was going to get himself killed if he hit loose gravel. "Keep up the fly-on-the-wall impersonation, and text me if anything changes before I get to town."

"Will do. Cameron plans to call you sometime this afternoon."

The SUV barreled toward her. Its grill reminded her of a monster baring its teeth.

Her stomach sank. The person intended to ram her. "Someone's going to hit me. Call the sheriff." Grace didn't hear Laura's response. Her focus had switched to survival. She slammed her foot on the accelerator. The truck lurched forward, putting distance between her and whoever planned to hurt her. Why would someone come after her? No one knew she'd taken Cooper's truck. She sucked in a breath. *He* was the target.

Grace fought against the gravel that tried to throw the truck into the ditch. The SUV rammed into the back corner of the vehicle. The screech of metal on metal pierced her ears. She gritted her teeth and fought against the pull of the wheels. Her futile efforts gave way, and the truck spun out of control. The entire episode happened in slow motion. Or at least that's what it felt like until the truck slammed into a tree. She smacked her head on the driver's side window. The seat belt latched and jerked her into the seat. The airbag blew, smashing into her face.

A haze swirled around her, and confusion knocked on her skull. What had…? Oh no. The entire horror show of what had happened settled in. Grace ignored the blood flowing from her nose over her lip and the lump on the side of her head. Her mission—get away from whoever ran her off the road and hope that Laura had called the sheriff. A quick glance confirmed her cell phone no longer sat in the cup holder. No time to search for it. She had to hide.

She pushed her shoulder into the door, but it didn't budge. Shifting around, she drew her knees to her chest and kicked out. The door creaked open a foot. She pulled back and jammed her feet into the panel once more. The sensation of a hot poker jabbed her leg above the knee. She panted through the initial pain. The size of the opening had increased enough for her to slip out. She squeezed through and fell to the ground. Staggering to her feet, she stumbled into the woods. Blood dripped from her face, down her shirt and onto the ground. First priority, get out of the line of sight from her attacker and then stop the bleeding. Or, at minimum, keep from leaving a trail. The pain in her leg decreased as she wound her way farther into the woods.

Ten feet into the cluster of trees, she paused and removed her jacket. She yanked off the long-sleeved blouse she'd worn over a T-shirt and wadded it under her nose. With one problem solved, she slipped her coat on. She refocused on putting distance between her and the driver and finding a place to hide.

Fallen limbs and roots grabbed at her ankles. Branches reached out, snagging her hair, ripping thin strands from her scalp. The adrenaline from the accident had faded, and her injuries sounded off. But her determination to escape long enough for help to arrive fed her energy.

The crunch of footfalls behind her spurred her on.

Who knew how long she'd scrambled through the woods. Exhausted, she stopped and tucked out of sight—she hoped.

Grace leaned against the tree trunk and attempted to slow her racing pulse. She didn't hear the person who chased her, but that didn't mean he'd given up.

Would Izzie and Cooper rescue her in time? Or would the person responsible for running her off the road find her and kill her?

Grace bowed her head and wished she believed in the power of prayer. She accepted that God was real but had stopped talking to Him years ago. It had never seemed to help. So, why would He listen now?

"Say what now?" Cooper used Grace's SUV as leverage to push his battered body to an upright position from where he'd been examining her flat tire and stared at his sister.

Izzie bolted down the front steps, her coat clasped in her hand. "According to my dispatcher Regina, a call came in for me that someone ran Grace off the road." She raced for her department vehicle. "Get in!"

Cooper held his ribs and sprinted to Izzie's SUV. He wrenched the door open a little harder than necessary. But in his defense, Gracie was in danger. He had no more than shut the door when his sister peeled away from the house.

Gravel spit from the tires, and the rear of the SUV fishtailed.

He clutched the grab handle and held on tight. "What did Regina say?"

"Grace's employee Laura called. Said she was on the phone with Grace when her boss told her to call me about someone trying to run her off the road." Izzie hit the end of the lane, whipped a right turn, and flipped on her lights and siren.

Worry gnawed at his stomach. Why had someone tried to hurt Grace? Had her action at Bateman's camper triggered the killer to come after her?

"I'm right, aren't I?"

He shifted to face his sister. "What are you talking about?"

"Lexi."

Here he was, tied in knots about Gracie, and Izzie wanted to talk about *that*? "Are we really going there right now?"

Izzie glanced at him, then refocused on the road. "Why not?"

"Oh, I don't know. Gracie's in trouble?"

"Humor me."

He wanted to do more than humor her. He unclenched his fist and took a deep breath to keep his mind from losing it. "Fine. Yes, Lexi is Grace's daughter."

"Lexi is obviously yours. You can't miss the family resemblance. But why does the family think my niece was Kaitlyn's?"

"It's a long story." He scanned the ditches on both sides of the road. Where had Gracie crashed?

"I estimate you have about five minutes to give me the short version."

"Or what? You'll tell mom?" The childish challenge left his mouth on reflex.

Izzie glared at him. "If I have to."

He gritted his teeth and continued to search

for his truck. "Nine years ago, Gracie and I took things a little too far."

Izzie snorted. "You think?"

"Knock it off. Bottom line. Grace gave Lexi up for adoption without my consent and disappeared. The social worker found me, and I took custody of my daughter. Kaitlyn and I started dating about a few months after Grace's and my time together. I never hid anything from Kaitlyn. She understood how hurt I was and the guilt behind it. When y'all assumed Lexi was Kaitlyn's, she offered to claim Lexi as her own, and I accepted. We decided to get married soon after Lexi came to live with me. So, we didn't correct you. Just let the family continue to believe what they thought. Besides, Kaitlyn was Lexi's mom in every other way." Cooper spotted his truck and pointed in the distance. "There. Up ahead."

"I see it. By Grace's nonreaction, I take it she doesn't know Lexi's hers." Izzie hit the brakes and skidded to a stop. "My personal weapon is in the glove box." She stepped from the vehicle and donned her jacket.

He grabbed the extra Glock and hurried to follow. "No. And she will not find out. And neither will anyone else. At least not yet."

"Copy that." Izzie pulled her weapon from her holster. "You take the right. I'll go left."

"Got it." They searched the truck and the surrounding area together like they'd been a team for years.

"I've got blood in the driver's seat and on the airbag."

"I have tire tracks leading away from the accident. Did the driver grab Grace and go?" His heart rate increased at the thought of the assailant kidnapping her.

"Follow me." Izzie motioned for him to join her.

"What is it?"

"Blood drops." She pointed at the ground. "They go into the woods."

"Do you think she got away?"

"That's the only thing I'm going to believe until we have proof it isn't true."

"If you're right, he must have heard you coming and ran." He appreciated his sister's philosophy. "Let's track her down."

The two moved deeper into the trees, where the drops disappeared.

"The limbs are crushed. I think she went farther in." Izzie's words gave him hope.

Cooper's body ached, but he ignored it the best he could and kept moving. They had to find Gracie.

From the evidence, Grace had zigzagged through the woods. She'd done an excellent job, but the disturbance of the leaves and the strings of blond hair highlighted her path. He and Izzie followed the trail back and forth through the forest.

Izzie held up a fist, and he halted without question. She pointed to a large tree about twenty feet away. An arm—barely visible—stuck out from behind the trunk.

"Cover me." Cooper strode with caution toward the person. "Gracie?"

Grace jolted to her feet and spun to face him. Blood covered her face and the front of her T-shirt. Her outer shirt lay balled on the ground, painted in blood.

"Cooper!" She stumbled to him and threw her arms around his neck, burying her face in his chest.

Her tears soaked his shirt. "I've got you."

"Cooper, please be careful." Her words were muffled.

"I'm more worried about you." He leaned back and cupped her face. He ran his thumb gently under her nose, wiping away the remaining blood.

She closed her eyes, and when she opened them, the agony was impossible to miss. "The rope. I was driving your truck. The killer is after you."

He scrambled to make sense of her broken statements. But he'd reassure her if that's what calmed her. "I'll be careful. I promise. Now, let's get you medical attention." He wrapped his arm around her waist and helped her walk through the woods back to Izzie's SUV, piecing together the meaning of her words. The crosshairs centered on him. But why?

His thoughts bounced from Gracie and what had happened to her, to the target that, according to her, appeared to be on him. Had he messed up, and the killer discovered the reason he started bull riding again? Or had the killer targeted him for an entirely different reason? Like his recent FBI case that turned into a tragedy.

THREE

With the help of his sister Payton, the rodeo's veterinarian, Cooper had wrapped his ribs to give him extra support. Between that and the prescription dose of ibuprofen, he might make it through the team roping event with Daniel. How he'd survive the bull riding tomorrow...well, that was beyond him. But at certain times, a person's life demanded the impossible. This was one of them. Catching a killer was infinitely more important than the discomfort from his boo-boos. Now, if he could only calm his racing heart that continued to beat ninety miles an hour after the incident with Grace earlier that day. The fact someone had hurt her, when it should have been him, hit hard. He'd never anticipated becoming the killer's target. Cooper searched his memory for where he might have slipped up and caught the guy's attention.

A large hand gently slapped Cooper on the back. He flinched at the pain even from the light touch. Turning, he saw his brother Daniel.

"Hey, man. Ready to ride?"

Not really. Especially after you whacked me on the back. Okay, so maybe not whacked, but it still hurt. "Sure. I'll do my part. You just take care of yours."

Daniel laughed. "Man, this is just like old times. You snarky and me my fabulous self."

"Har har." Yeah, Cooper admitted he missed competing with his brother.

"Gentlemen." Grace sidled up beside them.

"Where?" Daniel whipped his head around and burst out laughing.

Cooper jerked his thumb toward Daniel. "Don't mind him. He's in rare form tonight." He loved his brother's enthusiasm for life. At times, he wished he could be as carefree. But life hadn't played out that way for him. His job and the loss of his wife had weighed him down. Not that he had a bad life.

On the contrary, he had a great one. His daughter—proof of that. Sometimes, he just wanted laughter to come easy. Cooper shook his head. Did that even make sense?

"So, a normal night with my bullfighting partner." Grace smiled. She'd done a great job with the makeup she usually didn't wear at rodeos. The bruising around her eyes and nose had faded into the background. Thankfully, after the accident, the medics had confirmed she hadn't suffered anything serious.

"Exactly." Cooper rested his arms on the arena

fence and stuck the toe of his boot between the rails, getting comfortable, to watch Izzie barrel race.

Grace and Daniel mimicked his stance. However, Grace stood with both feet on the rails due to her height.

"How in the world did you talk Izzie into this?" Daniel asked.

"Meh, I have my ways." Cooper laughed. It was good to be home. He vowed right then to spend more weekends at the ranch once he and Lexi moved back to his home outside Lackard.

"Next up, our very own sheriff. Izzie Sinclair. She came out of retirement to barrel race at our annual Christmas Showdown." The crowd cheered at the announcer's introduction.

Izzie held steady, reining in her horse Firefly who pranced, ready to race.

Grace leaned over the fence and cupped her hands around her mouth. "Go, Izzie!"

The buzzer sounded. Izzie and Firefly burst into the arena. Her hat flew off as she approached the first barrel. She rounded it and let Firefly take off for the next one. The way his sister leaned into each barrel made his stomach flip-flop. But Cooper had to give her credit. She hadn't lost her skills. After the last turn, she bent forward over Firefly and sailed across the finish line.

He, along with Daniel and Grace, whipped their gazes to the scoreboard to see Izzie's time.

They whooped and cheered with the rest of the crowd. She'd come close to beating her own record.

Daniel whistled between his teeth. "Amazing. She might win this thing with that time."

"That girl is as good as she ever was." Cooper glanced at Izzie's time again. "Wow."

Grace cocked her head and lifted an eyebrow. "What are you two so shocked about? Izzie's always been the best in these parts."

"True," he and Daniel said in unison.

"You two are up in about forty minutes. Break a leg." Grace cringed. "Or maybe not after what happened last night. I'm going to congratulate Izzie, then find a seat with your mother to watch y'all team rope. See ya around." She jumped down and strode off to the barn.

"It's nice to have her back in town."

He shifted his gaze to Daniel. "Feels a bit like old times."

"Yup." Daniel's faraway look made Cooper wonder if his brother was thinking about his ex-girlfriend Annie. The man had never quite gotten over her. Daniel blinked and refocused on Cooper. "What are you *really* doing here? Taking up bull riding again—I don't buy it."

"Well, it's what I'm selling." Cooper narrowed his gaze at his brother.

Daniel's eyes popped wide. "No. You're kidding, right?" He leaned in and whispered, "You're undercover?"

Cooper blew out a breath between pursed lips. "I'm pleading the Fifth."

"Don't worry, man. I won't say a word. Does Izzie know?"

"What do you think?" He stared at Daniel, a little surprised Izzie hadn't informed the man of her plans since Daniel worked for her as a part-time deputy when he wasn't bullfighting and helping their mom at the ranch.

"I think if she didn't and were to find out, she'd clock you." His brother laughed like a loon.

He whacked Daniel on the chest. "Come on, little bro. Let's get saddled up and ready to ride."

Thirty minutes later, he and Daniel sat atop their horses, waiting for the announcer to call their names. One of the ranch hands, Garrett, hurried toward them.

Cooper braced against the saddle horn and leaned down. "What's wrong?"

Garrett grabbed Cooper's horse's cheekpiece. "Grace's SUV tire was sabotaged."

"Say that again?" No way had he heard the man correctly.

"The flat wasn't an accident. I took a close look at the tire. Someone stabbed it and then covered the hole. Whatever the person used as a plug must have fallen out while she drove to the ranch." Garrett's gaze pierced his. "Cooper, someone purposely made her tire go flat."

The truth gripped his stomach and twisted. "And if whatever they used to cause the slow leak hadn't dislodged prematurely, Grace would've been stranded on the country road in her SUV and not my truck."

"Yes, sir." The worry in Garrett's eyes mirrored his own concerns.

"Thanks for the information. I'll let Grace know."

"Next up, the Sinclair brothers, Cooper and Daniel." The announcer's timing couldn't have been worse.

"Do me a favor and go tell Izzie. Tell her to get eyes on Grace."

Garrett nodded and strode off.

"Everything okay?" Daniel moved his horse to Cooper's side.

"Not really." Since Daniel was not only his brother but worked for his sister, Cooper had no qualms about speaking his thoughts. "We thought someone had targeted me, but now I'm not so sure. Let's get this ride done as fast as possible. I need to find Grace."

"As if we do slow in this event. But I read you loud and clear." Daniel nudged his horse to the starting area.

Torn between jumping off his horse and racing to Grace or continuing with the rodeo, Cooper repeatedly tapped the horn on his saddle. If Grace hadn't planned to sit in the stands with his mother, he'd forget the event. But since she was surrounded by hundreds of people and with his family, he'd do his job and stay in character. She would be fine. He hoped.

He clicked his tongue and encouraged his horse to follow Daniel.

God, please don't let me make a mistake that causes her harm.

Grace eased through the barn. The cacophony of animal noises met her ears. She couldn't deny that she missed the camaraderie of rodeo life. She said hello to the cowboys and cowgirls tending to their horses and enjoying each other's company. She chatted with a few old friends and introduced herself to several newer, younger rodeo participants. Unable to curb her suspicious self, she examined each man through the eye of a PI. Could any of these men be on a killing spree?

Her boots clomped down the dirt path between the stalls as she scanned her surroundings, listening and looking for anything that proved the murder theory. From what they had deduced so far, Cooper's life depended on discovering the evidence behind the deaths. Between the frayed bull rope and someone running her off the road in his truck, worry had taken a foothold and refused to let go.

Grace touched her sore nose. The moment she realized she had to run for her life would be forever etched in her memory.

Frustrated she hadn't found a single piece of evidence but wanting to watch Cooper and Daniel compete, Grace wove her way through the building. Horses whinnied, begging for attention as she trekked by. *Sorry, boys, I can't stop and pet you right now. Maybe later.* She yearned for the unofficial equine therapy at Stone Creek Ranch. She missed her horse.

Never planning to return to Rollins for more than a quick visit, she'd long ago given her horse Harmony to the Sinclairs. Cooper's mom had graciously promised to take care of the animal for her. And anytime she wanted to ride, it would be hers. She'd never returned to the ranch. She longed for Harmony with a passion. But time had passed, and according to Izzie, so had Harmony a couple years ago. Grace swallowed the ball of emotion.

The cheer of the crowd intensified as Grace made her way to the stands, leaving the comforting sounds of the animals behind. She put a hold on snooping around the rodeo grounds and stayed within the buildings because she wanted to see Cooper and Daniel compete. That, and her mind wasn't at peak awareness after the accident. The throbbing in her head had lessened but hadn't disappeared. She'd be foolish to roam the dark parking lot without backup or someone knowing her plans. Instead, she allowed the information to rattle around in her brain, hoping to piece it together.

The fact someone had targeted Cooper confused her. How had he attracted the killer's attention during the first rodeo he competed in? She'd worked three, and the man responsible for four deaths hadn't surfaced until now. Granted, the entire case was based on speculation at this point. They had to have proof before Izzie launched a full investigation.

And then there was Bateman. His condition continued to bother her. The tests that had come back so far were inconclusive, and the doctors continued to wait on other results. The last time she'd talked with Laura, the man hadn't regained consciousness. Had the killer gone after two cowboys? No. That seemed unlikely. Maybe Bateman was the intended target, and Cooper's cover had been blown. That made more sense, yet not. Grace shook off the whirling thoughts and grabbed the handrail on the bleachers. The dirt from the arena floor and the familiar odor of the animals filled her nose. Some might think it annoying, but to her, it was soothing. She'd taken two steps up the stairs to sit with Cooper's family when the phone in her pocket vibrated. She pulled it out and read the text.

Luka: Meet me at Bateman's camper in five minutes. I have information.

Grace tapped the edge of her phone. What was Luka up to?

Grace: What information?

Luka: Not here. In person. And private.

Frustration warred with curiosity. If he had news, she couldn't ignore the request. She glanced at the arena and exhaled. Fine. She'd go and listen to what Luka had to say.

Grace: On my way.

Luka: See you soon.

Her shoulders sagged. So much for watching Cooper and Daniel team rope. She waved at Hannah, Cooper's mom, and Lexi, mouthed that she'd be back and slipped out of the grandstands.

She shoved her hands in her jacket pockets, hunched and drew the material tighter to keep out the chill. Her boots crunched on the loose gravel as she made her way to Bateman's camper on the edge of the parking lot. Why on earth would Luka have information? More importantly, how did he know to tell Grace? She froze. Her mind screamed at her that something didn't add up. But this was Luka, Cooper's friend. He'd never put Cooper in danger. And if what Luka told her protected Cooper? She decided in that moment to proceed with the meeting.

She shot off a text to Cooper and her employee Cameron.

Grace: Heading to Bateman's camper for new information.

She'd learned when starting her business to make sure someone always knew where to find her and what she was doing. The world of private investigations and security had plenty of unsafe situations. As a boss, she demanded precautions for herself and her employees.

With a quick scan of the area, she continued to the meet-up point with Luka. His request had an odd ring to it, but if she gleaned new information that protected Cooper, she'd go without question.

The camper sat quiet and alone—almost eerie. Grace inspected her surroundings. Even the normal low voices of cowboys hanging out in a truck bed were nonexistent. Strange. Her gut told her to wait for Cooper, but she'd known Luka for years. She trusted him. Good or bad? She didn't know.

Stepping lightly, she moved in silence toward the camper. "Luka?" Her soft voice seemed to echo through the night. She approached the temporary home and glanced to her left, then her right. Nothing. "Luka, where are you?" she whispered. Her phone buzzed. She read the text.

Luka: Come inside. I have something to show you.

The hair on her neck prickled. Why would Luka want her inside the camper? She assumed for privacy, but doubt swirled in her thoughts. She typed in a text.

Grace: Meet me outside.

Luka: I need your help.

What if Luka wasn't the man she thought him to be? No, nothing would happen. It was Luka—Cooper's best friend. Besides, the killer wasn't after her. He focused on bull riders, and at the moment, namely, Cooper. If Luka had anything that helped keep Cooper safe, she wanted to find out what he knew.

She turned the knob, opened the door and stepped inside. The lights were off. Not even the glow of a nightlight illuminated the interior. In that moment, she realized she'd made a mistake. A big one. She spun around.

Before she could escape, a hard object slammed into her head. She fell to the floor, and the world went dark.

Consciousness came at a sloth's pace. Unsure how long she'd been out, a minute or an hour, she coughed and coughed again. She waved a hand in front of her nose to ward off the offending odor and forced her eyelids open. Panic clawed at her throat. Flames licked the far side of the dwelling and crawled toward her. Smoke oozed to the ceiling, hovering above. She had to get out—now.

Her fingers wrapped the handle and pushed, but the door wouldn't budge. Using her shoulder, she put her weight into it. The door refused to give.

She glanced at the growing flames and scampered away, pushing herself to the far side of the entry. Her throat constricted. She coughed as the smoke thickened. She sat with her back to the outside wall, flung her arm out to the side and pounded on the door, screaming for help. But who would hear her in the deserted parking lot?

The foul air burned her eyes. Tears rolled down her cheeks. Drained of energy, she collapsed onto the floor. All her poor decisions slammed into her. Cooper would never know her secret. Grace would die, never being able to apologize for her mistake in judgment.

I'm sorry, Cooper. I'm so sorry.

Would God hear her pleas if she prayed? She wouldn't blame Him if He didn't listen since she'd all but refused to talk with Him over the years. But she had to try.

God, I could use your help. Please don't let me die before I tell Cooper about his baby girl.

FOUR

"Nice run, you two." Cooper's old friend met him and Daniel in the barn.

"Thanks, Luka." Cooper dismounted his horse. He scooped up his phone from inside the foot-locker where he'd left it and glanced at a text message from Grace. His gut twisted into a knot a Boy Scout would be proud of. "Have you seen Grace?"

Luka shook his head. "No, man. Last I saw, she was heading to the bleachers to hang out with your mom. Why?"

"She's not there." He shot a look at Daniel and handed his horse reins to his brother. "I need—"

"Go, find Grace. I've got Rascal." Daniel grabbed the leather straps and jutted his chin toward the doorway.

"Thanks." Cooper sprinted out of the barn. Even in the cool temperatures, sweat beaded on his forehead, and his stomach had landed at his toes. His boots kicked up dust as he hurried to Bateman's camper. The entire situation had bad

idea written all over it. Why hadn't she waited
for him?

Luka paced next to him. "What's going on?"

"I'm not sure…" His words hung in the air. The
smoke billowing from the camper stole his ability
to fill his lungs. "Hurry, Luka." Cooper poured
on the speed and skidded to a halt at the door. He
yanked his leather gloves from his back pocket
and shoved his hands in them. He grabbed the
handle and jerked. The door opened a few inches.
Smoke rolled from the small gap. Cooper covered
his nose and mouth with his arm and coughed.
"Help me get in there."

Luka wedged his fingers in the bottom. "Ready
when you are."

Cooper did the same from the top. "Pull!"

They ripped the door off the hinges and tossed
it aside. A wave of heat slapped Cooper in the
face. He grimaced at the intensity and nasty air.
Through the haze, he spotted Grace lying on the
floor to the right inside the entrance. He hopped
into the camper, scooped her into his arms and
bolted from the flames with his precious cargo.

"Put her down here." Luka had found a blanket in one of the nearby trucks and laid it down
a nice distance from the blaze.

"Call 9-1-1!" Cooper knelt and eased Gracie to
the ground. Her arms dropped limp to her sides.
He placed his fingertips to her neck, searching—praying—for a pulse. Air whooshed from

his lungs at the faint thump against his skin. He moved his hand to her nose. "She's alive, and she's breathing."

"Give me your phone."

Cooper lifted his gaze to Luka. "What?"

Luka held out his palm and wiggled his fingers. "Your phone so I can call for help. I misplaced mine."

He dug into his pocket, retrieved his phone and handed it to his friend. His attention returned to Gracie. There was not much he could do until the paramedics arrived except make sure she kept breathing. Luka's conversation with the 9-1-1 operator faded into the background. Cooper brushed the mess of curls from Grace's forehead and cupped the side of her face. Her thick lashes lay on her pale cheeks. She hadn't moved since he'd rescued her from the fire. "What were you doing out here alone, Gracie?"

"Here ya go, man." Luka handed him the phone. "The fire trucks and paramedics are on the way."

"Thanks." After his heart stuffed itself back inside his chest, Cooper scanned Grace for injuries. Soot smeared her face, and the grit on her arms made it difficult to assess for bruises. He lifted her hands and turned her palms up. A few scrapes and cuts but nothing serious.

Boots pounded, crunching on the gravel. "Coop!"

He tossed a glance over his shoulder. His sister sprinted toward the camper. "Over here, Izzie!"

She locked eyes with him and rerouted to his side. "What happened?"

Sirens pierced the night air. Help was coming. Cooper inhaled and coughed. The smoke had gotten to him, but not even close to what Grace had breathed in. "Not sure." He watched Grace's chest rise and fall, relieved her status hadn't changed. "I got a text message from her that stated she was heading to meet someone at Bateman's camper."

Izzie crouched beside him. "Anything else?"

"Did Garrett talk to you?"

"About Grace's tire?"

"Yes."

"He did. Do you think this has something to do with her getting run off the road?"

Cooper thought for a moment. "It's possible, I guess. But you're the law around here. I'll leave that up to you."

Luka didn't know the real reason Cooper had returned to the rodeo, and he refused to spill the secret. He shifted his gaze from Izzie to Luka and back.

His sister gave an almost imperceptible nod.

"I'll get on that as soon as Grace is taken care of." As if on cue, the ambulance appeared. "It's a good thing you and Luka got to her as quickly as you did."

"Yeah, smoke had filled the camper, and the

flames had eaten halfway through." Luka crossed his arms. "I don't know how she survived."

Had Cooper detected a bit of irritation in Luka's voice? No. Not possible. The situation probably rattled the man as much as it had him. "However it happened, I'm grateful we got to her in time."

The fire trucks rolled to a stop, and the ambulance parked a short distance away. The firefighters went to work, putting out the blaze while two paramedics dropped from the vehicle, grabbed their equipment and hurried over.

"What do we have?" the taller of the two asked while the other guy joined Cooper next to Gracie.

Izzie stood. "Hey, Tanner. Grace was in that camper with the smoke and fire. My brother Cooper and his friend Luka got her out."

"She's unconscious but hasn't stopped breathing." Cooper scooted to make room for the man his sister called Tanner. But he refused to let go of Gracie's hand.

The other paramedic dropped opposite Cooper, unzipped the medical duffel bag and removed supplies. "Did she inhale a lot of smoke?"

"I'm not sure how long she was in the camper before we got her out."

"We'll start with oxygen and see how she responds. But pending how that goes, we might have to intubate her to keep her airway from swelling shut. Name's Brady, by the way."

Cooper nodded and watched Brady place an

oxygen mask over her nose and mouth and listen to her lungs. The medics hadn't said it, but if they warned him of intubation, Gracie's condition must be serious. He closed his eyes and said a prayer for quick healing.

"Hey, Cooper, is it? The intubation warning was only to prepare you just in case. Her lungs sound good. I'm not worried."

"Thanks. That helps." At least a little. He appreciated Brady's attempt to ease his worry. But her limp body clawed at his heart.

"IV started." Tanner secured the tubing to Grace's arm.

Brady used a penlight and checked her pupils. "Huh."

"What?"

The paramedic lifted her head and examined the back of her head. "I think I've found the culprit for why she's unconscious."

"Well, are you going to keep us in suspense?" Tanner chided.

"She has a knot back here, and her pupils suggest a possible concussion."

Grace's pallor twisted Cooper's stomach. He'd never stopped caring about her, even after she'd almost destroyed him by her heartless move of not telling him about his daughter. But seeing her lying on the ground hurt brought back the old feelings he'd had as a teen. The ones that shouted she was *the one* for him. Until life fell apart.

He cleared the emotion from his throat. "That's why she isn't awake?"

"Between that and the smoke...yeah, that's my best educated guess."

For whatever reason, the preliminary diagnosis allowed Cooper to relax a bit. Not that smoke inhalation or a concussion couldn't be serious, but it explained the mystery. And he dealt with solid information better than the unknown.

Tanner and Brady moved Grace to the gurney and pushed it toward the ambulance. He spun to face Izzie and lowered his voice. "Tell Mom I'm going with Grace to the hospital and ask if she'll watch Lexi for me." Cooper scanned the surroundings. A small group of people had converged on the scene. "And you might want to do something about the crowd before they get wind of what's happening."

"I'll take care of it and talk to Mom. Go. Be with Grace. I'll meet you at the hospital later."

Cooper clutched Izzie's shoulder. He knew his sister would handle the speculation like a pro.

After a quick squeeze, he jogged to catch up with the paramedics and hopped into the back of the ambulance.

"I take it you're coming along." Brady rolled his eyes.

Cooper arched a brow. "Got a problem with that?"

"If the sheriff told you to come along, who am

I to argue?" The medic ignored his presence and continued to care for Grace.

He slipped his hand into hers and hung his head. *God, help Grace heal and help me figure out who did this to her.* The words stopped. What else could he do besides beg? Something he'd done throughout high school when her father had emotionally abused her. Cooper had guessed the man had left physical marks on her as well, but she'd never allowed him to see proof of his suspicions.

After he'd calmed down about her not telling him about their daughter and he could think straight, he'd deduced that her action in college of giving up Lexi stemmed from fear of her parents. Specifically, her father. One of the reasons he'd let go of the anger so quickly. Okay, maybe not quite that fast, but between Kaitlyn's coaching and his experience with Grace's father, the forgiveness had come. Now, to figure out how to broach the topic with Grace. He respected Grace's choice, but Lexi deserved to know the truth.

A coughing fit consumed Grace, shaking him from his thoughts. She rolled and clutched her middle.

"Easy." He brushed the soot-covered golden ringlets of hair from her face.

She panted. Her eyes fluttered open. "Cooper?"

"Right here, Gracie girl."

Her hand clutched his. The strength in her grip

amazed him. She batted away the oxygen mask. "Meeting. Setup." Her eyelids drooped closed.

"Someone set you up to come to the camper?" She nodded.

"Don't worry. Izzie and I won't stop until the person is behind bars."

"Sorry," she whispered.

"Nothing to be sorry for." He rubbed his thumb on the back of her hand.

"There is." She panted shallow breaths. "But later."

He placed his palm on her forehead, hoping his touch would calm her. "Okay, Gracie. Just rest."

The paramedic replaced the oxygen mask. "Just relax and breathe in the clean air."

"Wait." Grace removed the plastic from her nose and mouth. She made eye contact with Brady. "Cooper…permission…for medical care. Visitors, too." She wheezed.

Brady's gaze bounced to him, then to Grace. "Hold on. Let me record that since I'm the only witness." The medic pulled out his phone. "Okay, go ahead."

Grace repeated her instructions the best she could between coughs and short intakes of air, giving Cooper medical consent, then drifted to sleep.

Staring at the phone, Brady shook his head. "This is highly unusual."

"Smart move, by the way, videoing it." Cooper

had no doubt in his mind that her father might be an issue without the documentation.

"I hated to ask her to speak again, but I don't want there to be any doubt. With HIPAA regulations as they are, I'm covering both of us."

"I get that. And appreciate it."

"Any particular reason why?" Brady tilted his head and raised his brows in question.

"I have a good idea, but that's for her to say." He tightened his grip on her hand. *I've got you, Gracie. I won't let him hurt you.*

Brady nodded as the ambulance came to a halt. Cooper stepped from the truck and moved aside, allowing space for the paramedics to work. The emergency department double doors slid open, and a coordinated scurry of activity ensued. He followed the gurney inside and listened to medical jargon he only half understood. Grace and the medical staff disappeared down the hall.

Alone, he stared at the empty corridor. Now what?

He glanced at the waiting room. Red tinsel spiraled with white fairy lights swooped up and down across the large window on the far side. Christmas centerpieces decorated each small table in the room. The festive appearance did nothing for Cooper's mood. Worry clung to him like a stick-tight on a pair of wool socks. The whole scene was a little too cheery if you asked him.

A vacant chair near the nurses' desk called his

name. From that position, he'd be able to see the comings and goings of the room. His cowboy boots echoed on the tile floor. A woman with a small girl in her lap glanced at him, then returned to reading the little one a book. Cooper removed his Stetson and eased onto the seat. Hat hung on his knee, he rested his head against the wall and closed his eyes. His own aches and pains from the day before decided to make themselves known.

"Cooper."

He leaned forward and blinked at the paramedic standing before him. "How's she doing?"

Brady folded his arms over his chest. "The doctors say you rescued her in time. They aren't anticipating any lingering problems. And just so you know, they didn't have to place the tube down her throat, so I'm calling it a win."

The tension in Cooper's body deflated. "And her head injury?"

"A mild concussion. Nothing to worry about. A day or two of rest and she'll be fine."

"That's good." Cooper scrubbed his face with his hands. How long had he slept?

As if understanding where his thoughts had taken him, Brady smiled. "You've been asleep for about thirty minutes. Since Tanner and I haven't received another call-out, we stayed to monitor her situation. By the way, I showed the doctors the video of her consent. They noted it in her file. You're good to go on that front."

He nodded his thanks. "When will I be able to see Grace?"

"The nurses are in the process of moving her to the second floor. Head on up there. I'll let them know to keep you up to date." Brady turned and headed down the hall.

Cooper lifted himself from the chair and groaned. He was getting too old for this rodeo nonsense. He glanced at the door to the stairwell and shook his head. Nope. Not happening. He moved to the elevator and punched the button for the second floor.

Once settled in a more comfortable cushioned seat, his brain engaged. As far as he knew, Grace had no one other than her employees. He'd get ahold of her office and relay the message. Her parents were another story. How did he keep them from finding out? If Izzie kept Grace's name from the public, at least until the hospital released her, that problem would take care of itself. He hoped.

After getting his thoughts in order, he pushed to his feet to address the immediate problem. He strode to the nurses' desk. A small Christmas tree sat on one side, and strings of multicolored lights were draped in waves on the wall behind. Stockings with each nurse's name hung between the strands. The effect—calming.

"Can I help you?" Kathy, according to the woman's badge, smiled.

"I hope so. My name is Cooper Sinclair, and

I'm here for Grace Harrison. I'm on the medical consent form, and there should be a note that I have authority to deny visitors."

Kathy searched the desktop and grabbed a file. She flipped it open and scanned the document. "Yes, sir. Do you have any instructions?"

"Please do not allow any visitors unless I approve them first. That includes her parents." Hopefully, that would keep Arthur and Ava Harrison from causing problems. Either way, he'd protect Gracie from her old man and worthless mother. Not exactly the kindest way to refer to her parents, but sometimes the truth hurt.

She blinked at him like he'd lost his mind, then brushed off the look of confusion. "I'll let the others know."

"Thank you." Cooper tapped the counter with his knuckles and returned to the seat he'd vacated moments ago.

The murmur of voices from the nurses' station and the ding of the elevator, mixed with the occasional clunk of the vending machine, faded into the background as he sat and waited for word about the woman who was his daughter's biological mother and used to be his best friend. And according to his heart, the woman who had stolen the organ from the day they'd met.

The Mojave Desert had picked up roots and relocated to Grace's mouth. She swallowed, unsticking her tongue. At least it no longer tasted like an ashtray. Her ribs ached from coughing, but overall, she'd fared better than expected. From what she'd heard and the little she remembered, she had Cooper to thank for saving her life.

Nightmares of smoke and fire woke her several times during the night. Each time, she'd found the man her teen-self had fallen for sitting next to her bed. His soft snores had comforted her and gave her a sense of safety.

The hospital room's plastic-covered easy chair crinkled. Cooper. Her hero.

The corner of her mouth lifted, and she pried open her eyes. She sucked in a breath, kicking off another coughing fit. Her mother sat beside her bed. "What are you doing here?" Grace croaked.

Mom patted her hand. A sickening, sweet tone fell from her lips. "We're here to help."

Grace yanked her fingers from her mother's grip. The soft rhythmic beeps of the heart monitor to the left of her bed increased, matching the pulsing whoosh in her ears.

"I don't want you or your help." She scanned the room for Cooper. He never would've let them onto the floor, let alone her room, if he'd had an inkling they'd arrived. Even after all this time, she knew deep down that he'd protect her. "How did you get in here?"

"What did you expect? They'd keep your distraught parents out?" Her father stepped from the shadows and stalked toward her bed. "I'm smarter than you, little girl. Besides, that's what we do. We clean up after your messes." He gritted his teeth. "How stupid can you be? Getting stuck in a camper that's on fire. You're an embarrassment."

Grace pushed herself into the mattress. The memories of the bruises he'd left where no one could see them had haunted her for years after she'd fled from home to attend college. She'd vowed never to return to her hometown of Rollins for that very reason. "Go away."

"Listen here…" Arthur's hands spanned her ribcage and tightened like a vise.

She whimpered at the constriction.

"You selfish brat." He leaned in and whispered. His hot breath brushed her cheek. "You made a fool of us when you ran off to college, then the military, and didn't return. People questioned why. You humiliated us."

The pressure on her ribs increased. She cried out.

"Stop being a sniveling drama queen." Her father sneered.

Tears burned her eyes and pooled on her lashes. Nothing had changed since she'd escaped his abuse at eighteen. Why had she thought she could avoid him?

"You think I don't know about—"

The door slammed open, rattling on its hinges. Cooper's large frame filled the entrance. "Get your hands off of her." Cooper practically growled the words.

Her father released her ribcage and spun to face Cooper. "Listen here, you waste of oxygen. Hanging out with you, the bad boy in town, ruined my daughter's reputation."

Cooper stalked three steps into the room. He sucked in air through clenched teeth, fisting and unfisting his hands. Oh, the man was fuming. Grace had seen it before. The first time when his father's affairs came to light and the second, when he'd found bruises her father had left on her stomach. She'd denied what happened and had blamed it on a fall. But she was pretty sure Cooper suspected. Only without her admission he could do little about it.

"Mr. Harrison, I don't know how you weaseled your way past the nurses, but you and your wife are not permitted in Grace's room. Besides her, I am the only one with authority to allow you access." Cooper folded his arms across his chest. "And your access is denied."

"You have no right. She's our daughter." Her mother stood and circled the bed to stand next to Grace's father.

"I have every right." Cooper stepped aside and pointed toward the door. "Now, get out!"

Her father threw his shoulders back and glared at the man who saved her from more humiliation and pain. "This isn't over. Come along, Ava."

The pair strode past Cooper and out the door.

Tears streamed down Grace's cheeks and onto her neck. Silent sobs hitched in her throat. A habit learned out of fear from many years of repercussions if she made a sound.

"Aw, Gracie." Cooper's arms wrapped her in a cocoon of warmth and comfort. He palmed the back of her head and guided her to his shoulder. "I'm sorry. I stepped away for a minute. The nurses had an emergency while I was gone. Your parents must have waited until that moment to sneak in."

She nodded, burying her face in his chest and gripping his sleeve. Cooper's explanation sounded like something her father would do. Forbid the notion the man not get his way.

Cooper ran his hand down her hair over and over, calming her. "He's gone."

The plastic tubing from the nasal cannula tugged along her cheek. Wetness pooled on her upper lip. She lifted her head and used her hospital gown to wipe away the offending mucus.

"Here. Let me help." Cooper removed the breathing device and turned off the oxygen at the wall. "The nurses planned to take you off the air a few hours ago, but I talked them into waiting until you woke up." He plucked several tissues from the box on the roller table next to her bed and handed them to her.

"Thanks." She dabbed her eyes, then blew her

nose. "Sorry about falling apart on you." She inhaled, then pushed air through pursed lips.

"It's not your fault, Gracie."

"Maybe not, but I don't deserve your kindness."

His mouth opened, then closed. He rubbed the back of his neck. "Look, we haven't seen each other for years. We both messed up back then. But that doesn't mean I don't care what happens to you."

If he only knew how badly she'd botched things. She sighed. "I appreciate everything you've done. Saving me. Me shoving my medical care on you. How you handled my father."

"I admit it took me off guard, but I wasn't surprised." He slipped off the edge of the bed and onto the easy chair he'd occupied during the night. "I had Izzie notify your employees. They wanted to rush to check on you, but I convinced them not to. I hope that was okay."

"I'm sure Cameron gave you a hard time."

Cooper chuckled. "He did. I had to give him the full rundown of what happened. Along with the fact you were okay before he gave in and stayed away."

A smile tugged on the corner of her mouth. "Sounds like Cameron. What about Laura? She's here at the hospital, watching over Bateman."

"She peeked in on you last night to confirm my report." He rolled his eyes. "She's a spitfire."

A full smile bloomed. "That she is."

"Laura and Izzie have teamed up and compared notes."

Grace stiffened. Laura seen with the sheriff would blow her cover.

"Relax. Those two have it down pat. Izzie sat in the waiting room for me to give her an update. To pass the time, she struck up a conversation with a stranger—Laura. Izzie is known to be outgoing. No one will be the wiser."

"You have a point." Her tension eased. "Have they figured anything out yet?"

"Only that we have a problem on our hands. Nothing specific."

A knock on the door jerked Grace's gaze in that direction. Her heartbeat sped up.

Cooper leaned forward and rested his hand on hers. "There's no way your parents returned. Especially with me in the room."

"Come in." Her voice squeaked.

Cooper lifted an eyebrow.

Fine. She had overreacted. She cleared her throat and tried again. "Come in."

Izzie poked her head in. "Can I join you?"

"Sure." Having the Sinclairs by her side felt like old times. The best part—she could trust them. "What can I do for you, Sheriff?"

The scowl Izzie flashed at her was priceless. "Not funny, Grace."

"Actually, it is." She covered her mouth to hide her smirk.

With a dramatic eye roll, Izzie strode in, grabbed the hard plastic chair on the other side of the room and dragged it next to the bed. "How are you, my friend?"

"Overall, I feel pretty good."

"Gracie." Cooper narrowed his gaze.

"I do. Yeah, my ribs ache from coughing, my head hurts a bit, and my eyes are a little itchy from the smoke. But I'm breathing normally and thankful to be alive." And that was the truth. Had God heard her quick prayer and helped her? Maybe. A revelation to ponder for another time.

Seemingly satisfied with her answer, Cooper scooted farther back into his chair and crossed his ankle over his knee.

"I'm glad you weren't hurt worse." Izzie smoothed a hand over her tight ponytail and sighed. "I do need to ask you a few questions."

"I figured. Go ahead." Grace dreaded reliving the event, but it had to be done.

Izzie pulled out her cell phone, ready to type in notes. "What made you go to Bateman's camper?"

The *alone* was implied. Grace twisted her fingers in the blanket. The idea of hurting Cooper stabbed her heart. She'd done enough damage to the man. Although, he didn't know it—yet. "I received a text message asking me to come to the camper. The person had information for me."

Silence lingered. Izzie leaned forward, elbows on her knees. "From who?"

Her gaze drifted to Cooper, then to her lap.

"Grace, I need to know."

"Luka."

Cooper sucked in a harsh breath. "Not possible."

She shifted to face him. "I'm sorry, but it was from Luka."

"How do you know?"

Say what? "What do you mean, how do I know? My phone identified his number. His name popped up."

"Calm down, Coop. Let's go with the facts." Izzie refocused on Grace. "You received a message from Luka's phone asking you to meet him."

"Exactly."

"Did the messenger say or do anything to make you believe Luka sent the text other than the ID?"

Had he? She searched her memory. "No. I assumed Luka had sent the request. There was nothing to make me think otherwise."

Izzie shifted her gaze to her brother. "Cooper, can you confirm he didn't send the message other than your personal feelings?"

He ran his fingers through his hair, leaving the strands standing on end. "I guess not. But he didn't have his phone on him when we found Grace. He said he misplaced it and borrowed mine to call 9-1-1."

"That doesn't rule him out. But it doesn't confirm his guilt either. I'll do some digging." Izzie settled back onto the chair. "What happened next?"

Grace retold the event piece by piece. "The whole situation had leery written all over it. That's why I texted Cooper and Cameron. Well, that and I demand my employees report their locations at all times."

"Smart. And it's a good thing you did. I never would have known where to look for you." Cooper tapped his finger on his boot.

"Wait a second. I'm a little sluggish here. Why did you come to find me and not text me? There's no way you would have made it in time to get me out of the burning camper otherwise." The series of events happened too quickly for him not to have come running right after his ride and before he knew what was going on.

"One of the ranch hands, Garrett, stopped me to let me know we made a mistake. Someone tampered with your tire, Grace. I don't think I was the target. I think you were."

She swallowed the lump crowding her throat. "Me? Why?"

"We haven't figured that out yet." Izzie jumped into the conversation. "I suggest that once you're released from the hospital, we sit down and lay this case out. There are too many moving parts to make definitive conclusions."

"And with that said—" Cooper stood "—I'll go hurry the doctors along. But first, Gracie, I want you to come and stay at the ranch where we can protect you."

"Protect me?" Had he really just said that? "Did you forget what I do for a living?"

His shoulders drooped. "What I meant is I'd feel better if you had others around. I don't want your parents to find a way to wiggle themselves into your world again. Plus, if we're all together—" he pointed to Izzie "—then we can work on the case as we need to."

Grace scrunched her forehead. The man had a point. Especially about her parents. "As long as it's okay with your mom."

"Mom won't mind at all." Izzie smiled. "I'll even stay at the ranch house while you're there. That'll make her twice as happy."

The three of them laughed. Cooper and Izzie's mom cornered the market on all things motherly.

Izzie's phone rang, quieting the group.

"Sheriff Sinclair." Izzie's back straightened. "When?" Her eyes darted back and forth. "Cause? That's what I guessed. Thanks for calling." She hung up. "That was Doctor Martin. Drake Bateman passed away ten minutes ago. He had a heart attack. Aware of my suspicions, Martin ordered an autopsy."

"Heart attack at twenty-six years old? That makes no sense." Grace rubbed her temples. If she wasn't mistaken, the killer had succeeded in taking out another victim. And from what Cooper said, she was on the list of targets.

FIVE

Cooper padded through the ranch house in his sock feet, mulling over the events of the past twenty-four hours. All culminating with the death of bull rider Drake Bateman. Finding Gracie in the blazing camper had sent panic spinning through him. A possible attempt on his life, her as a target and Bateman as a casualty. How did it all fit together? Or did it? His protective side reared its head after he'd rescued Grace. His gut reaction? The whole mess set his nerves on edge. He'd experienced enough in life to heed the warning.

A quick glance out the kitchen window revealed nothing in the way of a threat. But he'd alerted the ranch hands to be on the lookout for anything out of place. If the killer knew about his and Grace's past relationship, the ranch might become a failed attempt at safety.

He returned to the living room where Grace had settled in the recliner several hours ago. "Here." He handed her a glass of water and a small plate with crackers and cheese and then sat on the couch near her.

"Thanks." She selected a piece of cheese and nibbled on the edge. "You know, you don't have to wait on me. Doc said I can resume regular activities as long as it doesn't cause my headache to get worse."

"I know. But yesterday scared me to death— scared everyone in the family. So much so that Mom is making your favorite snickerdoodle cookies. Let us take care of you for a while. It'll make us all feel better."

She shrugged and smiled. "I suppose. Just don't get used to it."

The scared young girl he'd once lost his heart to had morphed into a strong, independent woman. At least by appearance. The response to her father's words and actions spoke to an underlying fear she hadn't escaped. "Have you called your employees recently?"

"About an hour ago, while you took care of barn chores. Cameron played mother hen, which, by the way, he's terrible at." She chuckled. "Laura is mad that someone snuck past her and killed Drake." Grace waved a cracker in the air. "Not that the doctor confirmed murder, but we all suspect something of the not-so-legitimate variety when it comes to Bateman's death."

"Your employee has nothing to feel guilty about. From what I witnessed, she's very good at her job. If you hadn't told me, I wouldn't have tagged her as an undercover bodyguard."

"I'll pass that along. But from her perspective, it still stings."

"I understand that." Boy, could he. He'd played his last case by the manual, and what had happened? He'd killed the suspect in self-defense, but not before the man shot him in the leg. The incident had left him running through all the feelings. He hated taking another life, even if the circumstances warranted it. Then there was Lexi. The possibility of her losing both parents had terrified him.

"So…" Grace picked at the hem of her shirt. "I know you married Kaitlyn, had Lexi and then lost your wife, but what happened after…well, you know." Her shoulders slumped.

"After we both walked away?" That night, he'd allowed things to go too far, but he'd truly thought it would be the turning point for them. That they'd finally accept the attraction between them. Not a one-night-and-done thing.

Eyes down, she nodded.

"I met Kaitlyn and we got married. We struggled raising Lexi while I attended the FBI academy until I graduated. Then we moved to Denver, Colorado, where I worked at the local branch. When Kaitlyn died of pancreatic cancer four years ago, parenting Lexi alone seemed like an impossible task, especially as an FBI agent. So,

I requested a transfer to Lackard, Texas, to be closer to my family. The rest…" He shrugged. "Here I am. What about you?"

Grace huffed out a laugh. "A little over ten months later, I graduated college and joined the army to get away from my parents…and other things." She paused and pressed her palm to her chest. "I served my time as an army intelligence officer. I decided I didn't want a military career, so I moved to Lackard and opened my own business. I've kept my distance from Rollins until Donovan Keats, the rodeo director, hired me. I couldn't avoid coming home. And as you put it, here I am."

"Did you ever get married?"

"No."

"A boyfriend in Lackard?"

"I haven't dated since our night together."

"As in never?"

She met his gaze. "Not ever."

The pain in her expression crushed his heart. Had he done that to her? He scooted to the edge of the couch and clasped her hand. "I'm so sorry, Gracie."

"It's not your fault."

"I beg to differ." He should have protected her.

"I could have said no. But when you finally acknowledged you wanted to be together, it was a dream come true for me."

"Then I left for the FBI academy, and you disappeared."

Her eyes widened.

"The academy took up all my time for a few months. I tried calling at the first opportunity I had, but you changed your phone number. I even made a quick trip down a couple of weekends after that and discovered you'd moved."

"You did?"

"I figured if you'd done all that, you had no interest in seeing me again. So, I stopped trying." The hardest thing he'd done in his life.

"Daddy!" Lexi called from the other room.

He leaned back and turned his head in the direction of where she yelled. "What is it, princess?"

"Aunt Izzie's here!"

Cooper laughed. Why his daughter had to announce his sister's arrival was beyond him. "Send her to the living room."

"Okay!"

That girl. Spitfire didn't begin to describe her.

Grace smirked. "She's adorable."

His gaze met Grace's. *Just like her mom.* The thought hit him square in the chest. "A handful is more like it."

"So much for stealth." Izzie strolled in and plopped down next to him on the couch.

"Yeah, not with Lexi around." He snickered. "To what do we owe the pleasure of your company?"

"I'm sure you've heard, but Donovan Keats has

done the unexpected. He moved the bull riding to tomorrow. He said that there wasn't enough time to find a replacement bullfighter. He's hoping Grace is feeling up to working by then."

"No."

"Yes." Cooper and Grace talked over each other.

Izzie coughed to cover her laugh. "You two want to get on the same page and try that again?"

"There's no discussing it." Grace glared at him. "I'm ready now, so tomorrow won't be a problem."

"Gracie."

"Don't Gracie me. Look. I'm grateful you saved my life, but I have a job to do. The headache is minor, and I feel fine other than a few aches and bruises."

"I trust you to know what you can and can't handle." Izzie soothed the tension in the room. "But don't overdo it. The last thing I want is for my friend to get hurt worse."

Grace seemed to think over his sister's words. "I promise to be honest with you."

The dormant volcano inside him threatened to erupt. That simple statement sent his ire into orbit. Sure, she'd tell Izzie the truth, but she'd hid the most important person in the world from him. Why did it strike him like a sledgehammer now? He'd accepted it and moved on years ago. Hadn't he? Apparently not. Maybe having Gracie here with Lexi in the same house had triggered him.

He inhaled, settling his wayward thoughts, and brushed aside the odd reaction.

"Besides starting an argument, why else did you come?" Cooper asked before he said something stupid.

"I need a think tank. I've included Daniel in the know since he's one of my deputies, and he's already figured out that Cooper's undercover. He's fully up to speed. I've flown solo with this for so long, I could use your perspectives." Her eyes pinpointed Cooper, then Grace.

"I'll be happy to help." Grace's soft response kicked his protective nature into high gear. It might have been nine years since he'd had her by his side, but something about having her near had his feelings tangled in a knot.

"That's why I'm here." Cooper intended to solve the case before someone succeeded in killing Grace.

Wrangling in her runaway thoughts, Grace stared at the red poinsettia in the middle of the coffee table. She hadn't lied. Other than a few lingering aches from the car accident, she had no side effects from the smoke she inhaled last night. And the doctor said the bump on the head barely constituted a mild concussion. To the touch, it hurt like everything, but it wouldn't sideline her.

Cooper had swooped in and saved her—just like during their teenage years. He'd had a sixth sense about when her father *disciplined* her, and she needed to escape the evil in her home. She had a gut feeling that during those times, he'd encouraged Izzie to invite her over to hang out. And the way he'd stepped in at the hospital… People used to see him as the bad boy of the Sinclair clan. A love 'em and leave 'em type of guy, just like his father. But she knew the real Cooper, and the town's assumptions back then had been as far from the truth as a person could get. She'd never understood how the rumors had started. He'd always been her hero. And apparently hadn't given up that title even after nine years.

"Grace? What do you think?"

Cooper's question pulled her from the past. "Sorry, I spaced out there for a moment."

"Izzie asked if you think all four events—my fall, the accident, the camper fire and Bateman's death—are related."

"I'd like to say yes…but… I believe the fire and Bateman are connected, but I'm not sure about the accident or your fall from the bull." Cooper's cut bull rope gave her pause, but she couldn't lump it in with the other incidents. "Targeting two people, maybe, but three is risky."

Cooper scratched the stubble on his jaw. "I agree. At least one of these occurrences doesn't belong with the others."

"I'm here!" Daniel strode into the living room, arms out wide, a huge grin on his face.

"You're ridiculous." Izzie shook her head. "Get in here and act like a deputy, not the class clown."

"But you love me, and you know it." Daniel kissed the air.

Izzie's mouth twisted to one side, and she leveled a glare at Daniel that would scare a rabid dog.

"Fine." He flopped onto the other recliner, leaned forward and rubbed his hands together. "What did I miss?"

"We're discussing whether all the current events are linked." Cooper snagged a cracker from Grace's plate and leaned against the cushions.

Daniel lost his jovial demeanor. His brows pinched together. "I suggest we talk through each one."

"Start with Drake Bateman." Izzie conferred with her notes on her cell phone. "When no one saw him thirty minutes before the bull-riding event, his girlfriend went searching for him. She found him in his camper unconscious. No apparent wound. She called 9-1-1. He died later at the hospital."

"Did Doc ever figure out what happened to him?" Daniel asked.

"No. It's a bit of a mystery. Test-wise nothing has turned up, yet. But they did discover that Bateman died from a heart attack. The current theory is that he endured too much stress from whatever took him down. Doc Martin is wait-ing on the autopsy and additional tests, though."

Cooper's head bobbed up and down. His typi-cal *I see but I'm processing* movement. "Who had contact with him at the hospital?"

"I can answer that." Grace grabbed her phone and clicked on a text message. "Laura noted three of his cowboy friends, whose names are unknown since she isn't familiar with them, but she does have pictures of two out of the three plus some others. Bateman's girlfriend Macey. Two doctors and more nurses than she could keep up with." She glanced up from her phone. "Hospital secu-rity will probably have recordings of those who entered the floor. Laura's got a phenomenal mem-ory for faces. She could point out those that she saw enter Bateman's room."

"That's great." Izzie typed in notes on her phone app. "If the killer truly had Bateman in his crosshairs, the heart attack was deliberate."

"That's a big *if,* sis." Daniel kicked back the recliner and propped up his feet.

"We're just throwing out info and ideas right now. You can reel me in later."

Daniel clasped his hands over his chest. "Got-cha."

Izzie rested the phone on her lap. "I'll take the security videos and talk with the doctors. It'll keep the rest of you out of the spotlight. Grace,

I'd like to speak with Laura. Get her input and thoughts."

"I can arrange that." The weight of the investigation into a killer lifted. She wasn't alone, working in the dark anymore. "Cooper and I can question the girlfriend." She glanced at him, and he nodded. "I don't want to blow our covers, so we'll play it low-key."

"Perfect." Izzie smiled.

"So that covers Bateman and possible suspects there." Daniel's focus lasered on Cooper. "Why would someone sabotage your ride?"

"He's next on the killer's list. Someone unearthed that he's undercover. Someone wants him out of the competition." Izzie ticked each idea off on her fingers.

"Or he was the wrong target." Grace stared at Cooper. "You took Bateman's place in the lineup and the bull assigned to him."

Cooper stroked his chin with his thumb and forefinger. "It's possible. But how did *my* rope get cut? I didn't use Bateman's gear. Luka handed me mine when I arrived at the chute."

"Wait." Grace sat up straight and winced at the zip of pain from her bruises. *Don't move that fast again.* At least it wasn't her head that hurt. "Luka gave you your bull rope?"

"Yes."

"He's the one who texted me to meet him at Bateman's camper."

"No." Cooper swung his head side to side. "I don't believe it. He is not involved."

Izzie placed a hand on his forearm. "I don't want to think so either, but we can't rule him out. Not yet. Especially since he texted Grace."

"Why would he lure me to the camper and try to kill me?" Grace agreed that it didn't make sense that Luka would hurt her. But she wasn't ready to rule out Cooper's *accident*. "We can't ignore that he had your rope, and the text came from him."

"His phone." Cooper's no-nonsense tone hung in the air.

Grace whipped her gaze to him. "Excuse me?"

"The text came from his phone. Not necessarily him." Cooper sighed. "When we rescued you, he had to borrow my cell to call 9-1-1. He said he'd misplaced his."

"So he said." Daniel added the piece that supplied doubt.

"Daniel," Cooper scolded.

"I'm not saying Luka is guilty. But hear me out. What if he left it behind because he didn't have the opportunity to delete the messages?"

"I'm still not buying what you're selling. Luka was my best friend on the circuit. Why would he do this?" Cooper held his hands out.

"*Was* your best friend."

"Izzie, what are you getting at?"

"You two were inseparable, but you haven't

ridden bulls in years. Haven't ridden the rodeo circuit with Luka since you left for the FBI academy. Do you really know him anymore?"

Cooper's mouth opened and closed. "You have a point. Maybe."

"How about I do a little recon. He and Chris Reyes hang out now since they're the older riders. I'll talk with Chris and get a feel for what he knows. Then have a chat with Luka." Daniel held up a hand, stopping Cooper's comment. "I'll be discreet. If we decide he warrants a full interview, we'll deal with it. Until then, we treat him like a witness but with the eyes of him being a possible suspect."

Cooper tilted his head back and stared at the ceiling. "I guess I can live with that."

"Now. What about Grace's accident?" Daniel tossed the question out there.

The odor of loam and pine trees filled her senses. The terror of her attacker finding her in the woods strangled her ability to breathe. Not so different from how she felt when her father took out his disappointment on her. Not knowing if she'd survive the consequences.

"Gracie? Are you okay?" Cooper's soft concern pulled her from the depths of consuming fear.

"Sorry. I'm good." She inhaled. "I thought the person tried to run *you* off the road, considering it was your truck."

"That held water until Garrett discovered the

plug in your tire. I'd stake my reputation as an FBI agent that whoever ran you off the road had meant that accident for you."

"But why?" Grace closed her eyes and pushed on her lids. White streaks flashed against the pressure, but the building headache eased a bit. "Wouldn't the rodeo grapevine be alive if I'd blown my cover?"

"What if you stumbled onto something and threatened the killer's secret?" Daniel asked.

"I have no idea what that would be." She'd been careful not to ask too many questions while working or contact her employees until she left the rodeo grounds. No one should have known about her undercover assignment.

Cooper leaned forward and rested his elbows on his knees. "You said this is your third rodeo. Has anything happened to you at the other two? Something off?"

"No. Nothing." Her gaze connected with Daniel's. She'd worked with him since she'd returned. If anyone knew, it'd be him.

He shrugged and shook his head. "I didn't know until y'all told me, and I worked with her at all three rodeos."

"I did snoop around but kept it low profile."

"And this rodeo?" Izzie asked.

"My job as a bullfighter keeps me in the middle of the action. I don't have to sneak around." Until she did. She closed her eyes. "Bateman."

Cooper jerked his attention to her. "What about him?"

"When I heard about his accident...or whatever you want to call it... I hung in the shadows, gathering information and relayed it to Cameron." She swiped her hand over her mouth and made a fist. "That has to be it. Someone discovered why I'm here."

Cooper's brow pinched together. "Any idea who?"

"Not a clue. However, soon after I left the scene, I heard footsteps following me. I ducked behind a truck and waited for the person to leave. A few minutes later, whoever had paced the area walked away." Grace shivered at the memory of clutching her phone, her lifeline with Cameron on the other end. "Even before that, I got that itchy feeling of eyes on me. I have no idea who, though."

Cooper pushed off from the couch and strode to the window facing the pasture. He scanned the property as if searching for the killer. "Between that and being run off the road, I'd say someone pasted a target on your back." He yanked the phone from his pocket, punched a speed dial number and held it to his ear.

She glanced at Izzie, who sat stiffly with her eyes on Cooper.

"Garrett. Lock this place down. I want critter cams along the perimeter of the ranch." Cooper ran a hand through his hair, leaving it standing on end. "No, I don't want security cameras. We can't tip our hand like that. No one gets on this land without our knowing. Not even a family of raccoons." He listened for a moment. "Yes, that's perfect." Cooper hung up. His shoulders slumped. "The ranch hands will set up a rotation to monitor the ranch." He pointed at Grace. "You are staying here, and one of us will escort you anywhere you go."

Grace's respirations sped up. How had she exposed herself? Her gaze shifted to the window. A protest about him strong arming her sat on the tip of her tongue. However, she refrained. She might covet her independence and believe in her abilities, but she wasn't stupid. She nodded, accepting reality.

How had a simple investigation for proof morphed into a threat on her life?

SIX

Grace pushed the events of the past couple of days to the recesses of her mind and stepped into the rodeo barn a couple of hours before the bull-riding event. Her headache and lingering cough had disappeared that morning, allowing her to continue her job without worrying about permanent physical damage.

Dust particles suspended in the air danced on the fading rays of light from the openings that circled the animal pens. With each step, her cowboy boots and Cooper's kicked up small amounts of dirt. He hadn't left her side since they'd arrived at the ranch house yesterday. The entire family had taken care of her, including Lexi, who'd spoiled her with cookies and funny stories. Grace had rarely allowed her thoughts to drift to her baby, until she met Cooper's daughter. Now, her heart yearned for the child she'd never seen nor would ever know. Did the girl have her features or Cooper's? Or maybe a mix of both? No sense torturing herself. Grace shook off the longing and continued alongside Cooper.

"Hey, man. Glad to see you're back riding with us." Chris, Luka's friend and one of the older, more competitive bull riders, stopped and shook Cooper's hand. "And good to see you too, Grace. It's been a while. You and Daniel are our favorite duo out there."

"I appreciate the compliment. Glad I could step in and help for a few rodeos." She studied the man who had become a fixture in the rodeo scene for a moment and decided to go for it. "Did you hear about Drake Bateman?"

Chris lifted his cowboy hat and scratched his head before putting it back on. "Yeah, I did." He swept his hand in a flat arc. "We all did. Hard to believe." He glanced at Cooper. "Does your sheriff sister know what happened?"

How would he respond? Lie? Or tell the truth?

Cooper shook his head. "Nothing solid."

Well, that was the truth. Grace should have known he wouldn't give anything away. The man might keep things close and not share everything, but he didn't lie. Or at least, he hadn't when they grew up together.

"That's too bad. Bateman's girlfriend, Macey, is taking it hard."

"You've seen her?" Grace asked. The police had interviewed Macey after Bateman collapsed, but as far as she knew, the woman hadn't revealed anything useful. She made a mental note to talk with Macey herself soon.

"Sure. She came to collect Drake's gear. We chatted for a few minutes until she broke down and hurried out of the barn." Chris's shoulders sagged. "It's so surreal that Bateman is gone. We've lost too many over the year."

Grace forced herself not to react and noticed Cooper tucking away his reaction as well. "What are you talking about?"

"The bull-riding community lost Hank to cancer, Lance to a hunting accident, Brent to an overdose on painkillers, Ryan to a car accident and Barry to a heart attack. Now, Drake. We're all prepared for a life-altering injury from a bull throwing us or stepping on us—not that we dwell on it. As you're aware, we're a little cocky about our invincibility, but we know it can happen."

Cooper closed his eyes and nodded. No doubt his daughter, Lexi, was at the forefront of his mind.

Grace itched to gather him in her arms, but she'd relinquished that right the day she'd run away from him. With the untold truth a canyon between them, reclaiming the closeness would never be possible.

"I'm a bit surprised you returned to the action, being a single dad and all." Chris clapped Cooper on the upper arm. "But I'm happy you're back."

"Thanks. Things have changed in the community. Lots of young riders. You've got to admit—we're the old guys now."

"Old. Man, you know how to make it hurt." Chris laughed. "But, yeah, we're the experienced crew. That's why I'm shocked you returned to competition. Even if it's only for the promotional rodeo."

"I'm just trying it on for size. My last FBI case shredded me." He massaged his thigh. If Grace had to guess, she'd say he did it subconsciously.

Chris bobbed his head. "That's rough, man. And what about you, Grace? I hear you own your own business."

"That I do. But when Keats called for a favor, what was I supposed to do? The guy's persuasive." She shrugged.

A deep belly laugh filled the air. Chris patted her on the back. "Ain't that the truth."

"How are the new riders? I've met a few over the last few rodeos, but I don't really know them." Grace threw out the question, praying Chris had insight into the group of men.

The man scratched the stubble on his jaw. "Well, as the FBI man said, we're the old guys. Me, Luka and now Cooper. Petey is finding his way. Jamison is good and the nicest guy you'll ever meet. He has some serious potential. Billy, on the other hand, is...shall we say, competitive."

Cooper stood taller. "Billy? I don't recall a Billy."

"Not his real name. We call him Billy when

we all hang out. You know. After the singing big mouth Billy Bass."

"Come again." Grace knew about the singing fish, but why the nickname?

"Not only does that kid sing karaoke at any opportunity he gets, but fishing is his second love next to bull riding. Ergo, the name Billy." Chris held out his arms, palms up.

"Got it." Grace jolted at the pressure of Cooper's hand on the small of her back.

Tension rolled off him. "What's his real name?"

Chris shrugged. "Honestly, I'm not sure. I don't pay attention to the announcers unless it has to do with my ride. The last name is Murphy, though."

"I don't think I've met him." Grace made a fist and tapped Cooper's hip. "I'm sorry, Chris, but we need to get moving. I have to get ready for bullfighting and all that."

"It's great to have you and Daniel playing catch out there, Grace. Cooper, I hope you plan to stick around." Chris spun on his boot and swaggered away.

Grace shifted and gripped Cooper's arm. "What is it?"

He jerked his head toward a corner away from listening ears. Once there, he scanned the area.

"You're worrying, me. Spit it out."

"Before my first ride, I overheard a cowboy talking to Billy. Something about not making it obvious."

"It? What were they referring to?"

"Beats me. But now I'm wondering if this Billy guy tampered with my rope or is responsible for Bateman's demise."

"Or both. But why?" The hair on the back of Grace's neck stood straight. The sensation of eyes on her sent a shiver ripping across her shoulder blades. She grabbed his bicep.

"What is it?"

Her gaze raked across the barn from where they tucked into the corner. She tightened her grip. "Do you feel it?"

"Someone watching us?"

"Yes." Her pulse rate kicked up a notch.

"Maybe they think we've reconnected."

"Then let's make it look that way." She lifted on her tiptoes and leaned in.

The moment her intent clicked, his eyes widened.

She placed her hands on his shoulders and almost laughed at his expression.

Feet shuffled behind them.

Cooper dipped his head. His lips brushed against hers. Not a full kiss, but the touch had memories and regrets flowing through her.

"Oops, sorry," a male voice said and shuffled away.

The barely there kiss ended, but neither she nor Cooper moved.

"I…um…it was the only thing I could think

of…" Her heart threatened to leap from her chest. Cooper hadn't changed. He was still her safety in the rocky storms. Her life—a struggle, yes—but it could have turned out so different if not for him. She owed him the truth about their baby.

"Don't apologize." He tucked a strand of hair behind her ear.

"I'm not. But Cooper, there's something you should know." Now wasn't the time. They both had to focus on the bull riding event coming up. "Let's talk after—"

"I knew it."

Grace spun and faced the last person on the earth she wanted to see—her father.

"You had to hook up with the Sinclair bad boy—again." The snarl on Arthur Harrison's lip made her want to gag. She'd witnessed it too many times and experienced the consequences that came with it.

Cooper tucked her behind him and folded his arms across his chest. "Why are you here?"

"Not that it's any of your business, but I came to extract my daughter from this foolishness. She's embarrassing herself by pretending she's a bullfighter. Not to mention her ridiculous business." Arthur flicked a piece of hay from his shirt and pinned her with a dagger stare. "Quit fighting me, little girl. You'll regret it."

Her blood pressure galloped out of control. She bowed her head, unable to control her reaction to her father's demands. It didn't matter that she was thirty-two years old and a successful business-woman. The conditioning from her youth continued to linger.

"I suggest you turn around and walk away, Mr. Harrison." Cooper practically hissed the words.

"Or what? You're a player just like your father and a loser. You left your FBI career behind when it got hard and came back to play around at the rodeo." Arthur tsked. "I will not allow you to take my name—my daughter's name—down with you."

"Oh, I think you had it right the first time."

"Excuse me?" Her father's brows rose.

"It's all about you. Your name. It has nothing to do with Grace."

"That girl has been nothing but trouble from the day she was born." Arthur clenched his jaw and shifted to pin her with a glare. "I'll deal with you later." With that, he spun and marched off.

She swallowed—hard. At fifteen, Arthur had almost killed her. In his fury, he'd wrapped a cloth around her throat and strangled her to the point she'd passed out. He'd locked her in her room for days, ensuring the marks on her skin faded before allowing her to return to school. She'd never told a soul about that night. Not even her mother, who had been visiting her childhood best friend during that week.

Cooper faced Grace and tugged her close. "Don't go anywhere near that man. I don't trust him."

She rested her forehead on his chest and filled her lungs. *Neither do I.*

God, if you're listening, please don't let my father hurt me again. Her request might be a plea in the wind. She and God still felt miles apart, but desperation did funny things to a person.

Cooper's body buzzed with rage. He'd known deep down that Grace's father had emotionally abused her and suspected physical abuse as well, but she'd never confirmed the latter. The failure to protect her would always gnaw at him. He should have stepped forward, but without proof, his accusation could have triggered the man, and Grace would have paid the price. He refused to allow her father to get his claws into her again. Or anyone, for that matter. Her father or the killer.

He rubbed small circles on her back, giving her a minute to collect herself. "Time to get ready for the bull riding."

She nodded against him.

"Are you going to be able to work the event?" The appearance of her father had shaken her. He worried she wouldn't be able to shove the confrontation aside and focus on doing her job. Lack of focus in the arena could get her hurt.

"I'm good." Her voice was muffled against his shirt.

"Are you sure?"

After a deep, shuddering breath, she pulled away. "I'm not going to let my father control my life." The implied *anymore* had come across loud and clear.

The corner of Cooper's mouth tugged upward. "You realize we might have started rumors."

Eyes closed, she chuckled. "Wouldn't be the first time in our lives."

When her vulnerable blue eyes fixed on him, the rage toward her father, the hurt from her untold secret about their daughter and the anger aimed at the killer melted away, replaced by a desire to shelter her from all the evil in the world. "Let people think what they want. Anything between us is just that—between us."

She stared at him for a moment, then patted his arm and nodded. "Come on, cowboy. You have eight seconds on the back of a bull to survive."

He tipped his head back and groaned. "Thanks a lot for that reminder." Cooper jerked his chin toward the main part of the barn. "Come on."

The pair strode to Grace's locker, where they found Daniel sitting tying his cleats. He finished and stood. "Good. You're here." Daniel pointed at Grace. "You've got work to do."

She examined his attire and rolled her eyes.

"I see we're going with fun for the finals. Good thing I packed my gear."

Cooper had missed the camaraderie between these two. During the years Grace and Daniel had worked together, they wore the basic black baggy knee-length shorts with a standard shirt, but when finals arrived, the pair chose to wear a colorful outfit and a bit of clown makeup. It appeared Daniel had decided to continue the tradition. Cooper aimed his attention toward his brother. "Have my stuff?"

"It's in here." Daniel patted the container. "I'm the only one with the key."

"Thanks, man." Cooper lifted the lid and retrieved his equipment. "Have you talked with Luka yet?"

"He arrived a few minutes ago. I'm assuming he's gearing up for his ride." Daniel adjusted the colorful suspenders he had saved for finals. "Whatever you do, don't tip him off. We're looking into him."

Cooper snorted. "Not my first rodeo, bro."

Daniel laughed like a loon. "No, I guess it's not." His brother turned serious. "Stay focused and be careful out there."

"Lexi." His daughter—his entire reason for not getting overconfident or taking risks with his life.

"Enough said." Daniel grabbed his cowboy hat and plopped it on his head. "Ready to go, Grace?"

The white around his mouth gave him a perpetual smile.

"Almost." She tucked away the basic makeup, secured her footlocker and slung an arm around Daniel's shoulders. "How do we look?"

Cooper shook his head. The two intended to revive the fun act they saved for the finals. Neither played the part of a rodeo clown, but the crowd enjoyed the transformation from a regular bullfighter to the colorful and playful outfits and the bit of silliness the pair threw in for the special night.

"You guys look—" he rubbed his thumb and forefinger along his chin "—ridiculous."

Grace grinned. "Mission accomplished."

He moved close and whispered in her ear, "Be safe, Gracie."

"Back at ya, cowboy." She tipped her cowboy hat and strode to the arena.

"She's something else." Daniel watched her disappear around the corner.

"That she is." Cooper hefted his ropes over his shoulder. "But there are things you don't know, so lay off the matchmaking."

Daniel slammed his hand over his heart, feigning insult. "Now, would I do that?"

"Yeah, ya would. Now, get out of here and go save my hide."

"I have my catcher's mitt ready." His brother's

laugh echoed in the barn as he jogged to join Grace.

Time to get his focus on. The last thing Cooper wanted was to make a stupid mistake and get seriously hurt. He'd barely escaped a grave injury a couple of days ago.

"Hey, dude!"

Cooper shifted.

Luka hustled to his side. "Ready to kick some bull bootie?"

"You know it. I've missed this." And he did. Although, he had no intention of continuing after they arrested the killer. The risks were too high. Sure, the FBI wasn't without danger, but he had more control over those hazards of the job. A two-thousand-pound animal? Not so much.

"I, for one, am glad you're back." Luka tilted his head toward the arena. "Let's get you ready. You're up third."

He blew out a quick breath. "Eight seconds. I've got this."

"Yeah, ya do." Luka pushed him forward. "Go show these young'uns how it's done."

Cooper shook his head, and while he waited his turn, he wondered, not for the first time, why he'd agreed to this craziness.

He checked and rechecked his gear before climbing onto the bull. At least this time, he'd pulled a less experienced bull than Vortex. Adjusting his rope, he settled in, nodded his head and the chute opened.

For eight seconds, he held on. When the buzzer went off, he dismounted and jogged to the gate. The crowd cheered, and Daniel and Grace handled the bull like pros. Cooper accepted his ropes from one of the pickup men and headed for the exit gate.

His smile widened when his score hit the board. A cheer rose in the arena. Even a little rusty, he still had it. He waved at the crowd and tipped his hat. After putting his equipment away, he joined a group of cowboys at the fence and positioned his elbows along the top. With his bull-riding job complete, he took several calming breaths and settled in to enjoy the rest of the event.

As cowboy after cowboy finished their ride, the audience laughed and cheered at Daniel and Grace's antics. Cooper enjoyed the silliness along with everyone else, but he never let his guard down. He scanned the bleachers and the surrounding area, staying alert. Looking for any threat against Grace.

Next to last, Luka entered the chute and went through his preparation routine. Cooper watched from the spot at the fence and threw up a quick prayer for his friend's safety. Luka's chin bobbed up and down. The gate opened. The bull took its job seriously, bucking and twisting.

Cooper caught a glimpse of Arthur Harrison in

the stands. The man hated bull riding—hated rodeos in general. He claimed the sport was beneath him. So why was he here? Cooper refocused on Luka in time to witness his friend fly from the bull and land with a thud on the ground.

Daniel and Grace went to work. Daniel sprinted to Luka and helped him to his feet while Grace waved her red and yellow scarves, distracting the bull. Cooper gripped the rail as he witnessed the bull charge Grace. He'd forgotten the heart-pounding effect watching Grace do her thing had on him.

She sprinted to the barrelman barrel and vaulted in. A second later, Grace jumped out and stumbled toward the fence as the bull lowered his head and rammed into the barrel. The contact splintered the barrel. Pieces rained down all around her.

"Grace!" Cooper vaulted over the rail. Dirt kicked up from his boots as he fought to reach Grace, praying he'd make it in time to protect her from the angry bull.

He skidded to a stop next to her. The pickup men had taken care of the bull, and Daniel had Luka. Cooper wrapped his arms around her and breathed deeply. His gaze drifted to where he'd seen Arthur. The rat had disappeared.

Cooper closed his eyes and cradled a shaking Grace to his chest. The thought of losing her crashed into him. The hurt and anger of the past no longer held him captive. He had to come clean about Lexi and accept her response. No more hiding the truth. But for now, he'd let the relief wash over him. She'd had too many narrow escapes. What if he couldn't protect her from whoever had her in their sights?

SEVEN

The rhythm of the body brush as Grace groomed Jasmine, one of the horses at Stone Creek Ranch, calmed her nerves after the near-fatal incident at the rodeo. The moment she'd jumped into the barrel and realized someone had tampered with it, along with the whack of the bull hitting the barrel, sending pieces flying through the air, would forever be etched in her memory. A shiver raced up her spine. Was she safe anywhere? Her gaze scanned the interior of the barn. The Christmas decor Lexi had added to the stalls was a contrast to her jittery nerves.

Even with all the precautions Cooper had put into place, what if the killer found her on the ranch? A tiny meow shook her from the unease. She rested her cheek against the horse's, soaking in the unconditional love, finding the peace she'd experienced before her trip down memory lane.

A small orange cat wove through the bales of hay and hopped onto the ledge of the stall. The soft mew added to the tranquility of the barn and the animals within. She ducked under the horse's head, then ran a hand down the cat's back and swooped up his tail. The furball's motor went into high gear.

"You're a happy one, aren't you?" Her question received a nose bump from the feline. "I see how it is. You're an attention hog." Grace scratched under the cat's chin and returned to Jasmine who nudged her side, demanding she continue the brushing job.

Cooper had brought her to the ranch an hour ago. She'd showered, changed clothes and escaped to the barn soon after. Grace missed the serenity of her safe space, the soothing action of working with the horses and the soul-restoring peace that engulfed her when she visited the ranch. The attempts on her life aside, one thing in her past refused to quiet. The truth she'd held from Cooper for the past nine years.

Tears pooled on her lashes. "What do you think, Jasmine? Should I tell him?" Ever since the latest close call on her life, she battled the guilt and regret she'd stuffed down for years, ignoring God's prompting to search out Cooper and tell him what she'd done. The thought of leaving this world without spilling her secret to Cooper soured her stomach. She'd become desperate to relieve the chasm between them. Between her and God, and her and Cooper. Cooper deserved to know. Even if he hated her for the rest of her life, however long that would be with the threat hanging over her. She swiped away the single tear that found a path down her cheek.

"Gracie?"

She sniffed and wiped her face. When she moved under Jasmine's head to face Cooper, her breath caught in her throat.

Concern swam in his eyes. "Are you okay?"

The answer *I'm fine* sat on her lips but never fell. Who was she kidding? The latest close call had rattled her. "I'm…processing."

His boots struck the floor as he strode across the barn and stopped in front of her. He skimmed his fingers down her arm. "I'm not going to lie. What happened earlier scared me to death. If you hadn't noticed the barrel had been tampered with, you could have…" He cleared his throat.

"Please, don't. I just want to forget about it."

He raised a brow. "Do you really think we can do that?"

"No, but for now, please let it go. At least for tonight." She'd relived it twenty times in her mind since Cooper had covered her with his body, sacrificing himself for her.

He dipped his chin to match her eye to eye. "Want to tell me why you escaped out here?"

"You know me and horses. They're my comfort animals."

"I remember." He tucked a loose strand of hair behind her ear.

The caring touch brought her guilt front and center. "Cooper, we need to talk."

He tilted his head and studied her. "Then let's go sit over there." He motioned to the bales of hay placed along the wall. "Not exactly a couch, but it'll do."

Grace placed one foot in front of the other, forcing herself to move. She had to tell him about the baby she gave up. If the attempts on her life had done anything, they had clarified her life—the achievements, the mistakes and the reasons. Sitting on the bale, she plucked a piece of hay and ran it through her fingers. How did she tell him? Where did she start?

Cooper straightened his legs in front of him and crossed his ankles. "Gracie? What's going on?"

Christmas lights twinkled over each stall. A contradiction to her mood. "I hadn't planned on ever telling you, but now after seeing you with Lexi… Over the past couple of days, I've realized how wrong—how selfish—I was." Emotions clogged her throat.

"We were best friends growing up. You know you can tell me anything."

You'll hate me after you find out. She dipped her chin. "I don't know where to start."

Cooper slid his hand into hers and squeezed. "Why don't you start at the beginning?"

She huffed out a humorless laugh. "That would

be the day I was born." Life had never been normal. For as long as she remembered, her father hadn't loved her. No, that wasn't quite right. He had hated her. But why?

"You're referring to your parents, more specifically your dad, aren't you?"

The comforting scent of hay and horse filled her senses. If only it were that easy. "I don't know what I ever did to him, but yes, I could never make my father happy. Always a disappointment no matter what I did. And mom seemed to be oblivious, or maybe she didn't care." Grace shrugged. Over the years, she'd tried to figure out why her mother hadn't stepped in to protect her but had given up. "You and Izzie inviting me to spend time at Stone Creek Ranch saved my sanity."

"Izzie and I knew things weren't right. Anyone with a brain knew he emotionally abused you. I never understood why your mom didn't stand up to him and save you from the pain. I always suspected it was more than psychological, but you hid it well. I couldn't prove it." Cooper pulled in his legs and sat straighter. "Your father physically abused you, didn't he?"

Tears streamed down her cheeks. She hadn't allowed anyone, including her best friends, to see the evidence of his assaults. Of course, her father had left the bruises in places easy to conceal. But Cooper knew. She knew that deep down he'd always known. "I never told because I didn't want to make it worse."

Cooper blinked, then his eyes widened. "The week you missed school. You were always at school. Even when you were sick. What happened that time? What did he do?"

Surprised Cooper had zeroed in on that instance, she struggled to find words. But she'd vowed to herself to open up and tell him everything. "He strangled me. Almost killed me." Her hand brushed her throat. Phantom pains throbbed beneath her fingers. "He threatened me to stay silent and forced me to remain at home until the bruises healed."

Cooper sucked in a breath. "Because of me."

She twisted to face him. The distress in his eyes would have taken her to her knees if she'd been standing. He realized what had caused her father's anger. She nodded.

"I'm so sorry." He rubbed the back of his neck.

"It's not your fault. I was a willing participant in our first kiss. The fact my father walked in on it…well, let's say it was bad timing."

"Arthur never minded you hanging out with Izzie, but when he thought you and I, the town's bad boy—" Cooper used air quotes around the description "—had hooked up, he lost his mind. He hauled you out of here, chastising both of us and warning you not to kiss me again. I suspected he'd abused you, but I didn't have proof. Why didn't you tell me?"

She clutched his hand and held it tight. "Think about it, Cooper. If I'd have told you or your family, you'd have told the cops."

His forehead scrunched. "Of course we would have."

Grace held up the hand not holding his. "That's just it. What if they didn't charge him? What if I had to go home and face his rage?"

Cooper tipped his head back and closed his eyes. He expelled a long breath. "I get it. I do. But I don't like it."

"The same way I didn't like people talking bad about you. You let everyone in town believe you were a player like your old man. I don't understand why you didn't speak up and defend yourself."

He dropped his chin to his chest. "When Dad cheated on Mom, and she finally kicked him out of the house, us kids had no idea how to handle it. Dad had always appeared larger than life to us—to me. He was my hero. Until he wasn't. The hurt in here—" he patted a hand over his heart "—was too much. At seventeen, I had no idea how to deal with that kind of emotional pain. I dated several girls over the next few months, and the rumors started flying that I was like my father—a player. So, I kicked it up a notch. Whether or not it was true, if the people in town were going to accuse me of being the local bad boy, I might as well live up to it."

"You could have proved them wrong instead." She rested her hand on his arm.

"By then, I'd given up trying to save my reputation, which should never have come into question. You always saw me for who I was and not what others had tagged me as." He laced his fingers with hers. "I'm sorry I didn't save you from your father."

She shrugged. "You left for the rodeo circuit, then college, and I kept my head down in my schoolwork. I isolated myself so that dear old daddy had nothing to punish me for." She shook her head. "Summers were another story. I continued bullfighting with Daniel. I made money that I squirreled away and got to spend time with my rodeo friends. Trust me, Arthur Harrison did not like his daughter hanging out with the riffraff. Those months were difficult, but I could use my job to explain the bruises."

Cooper's eyes drifted to the ground. "I wish I'd have known."

"I lived through it. I left for college, and because of my stockpile of money, I never returned."

"Then I showed up on your doorstep."

"And that's where the story continues. I was so lonely. Sure, I dated and had a few friends, but the relationships were superficial. I missed you so much." She swallowed the emotions threatening to bubble over. "I craved to be loved but wanted no one but you. Then suddenly, you were standing at my college apartment door."

"When I saw you, I realized you were my everything. I'd ignored my heart. I didn't think I was good enough for you." He closed his eyes. "When you opened the door and threw your arms around me, I knew you were it for me. Then I took it too far and ruined everything."

"I think we are both responsible for what happened."

His warm palm cupped her cheek. "But I scared you off."

"No, you didn't. The consequences of our actions did." Grace couldn't hold it in any longer.

"Explain."

She blew out a long, slow breath. This was it. Time to release the truth. "I messed up. And as much as I'd like to, I can never fix my mistake. I only hope that someday you'll forgive me."

Cooper clutched her shoulders and dipped his head so they were eye to eye. "Tell me."

Sweat beaded on her forehead. She could do this. Tell the truth and pray for the best. God had listened earlier, maybe He'd help her now. *God, You've wanted me to do this for so long, and I've ignored You. I'm not ready, but with Your help, I can do this. Please help Cooper understand.* "That night we spent together, I got pregnant."

He sucked in a ragged breath, but his gaze stayed glued to her. "The baby?"

"I gave her up for adoption without asking you. As much as I hated my father, I couldn't be a disgrace to my family. To live through his wrath again. But more than that, there was no way I'd allow my little girl to be near him—for him to destroy her like he'd done to me."

"You could have told me. I would have helped you." The hurt in his tone shredded her heart.

She closed her eyes. "I'd felt horrible that I had taken away the opportunity for you to know your baby girl. But when I saw you with Lexi and what a wonderful dad you are, it hit me hard. I had done more than hide the truth. I cheated you out of your daughter."

Cooper shot to his feet and paced a five-foot strip in the dirt, fists clenched at his sides. The anger and rage that surfaced surprised him. He'd expected the admission—had even waited for it—wanted it. So why the visceral reaction?

He whipped his phone from his pocket and checked the surveillance cameras around the property. Grace in the barn by herself had worried him, but he'd monitored the area, giving her alone time. Now, he needed the time to compose himself and confirm her safety.

"I'm sorry." Grace's soft words echoed in the barn.

When the social worker contacted him eight years ago, it had taken his wife, then girlfriend, to talk him out of tracking down Grace and demanding answers. Months later, he'd held his precious daughter in the middle of the night. He let go of the resentment and had forgiven Grace. He couldn't believe, after all these years, that the deception had the ability to cut him so deeply. He'd wanted this—her confession—since the day he'd discovered his daughter.

"I don't know what to say." His mind spun to a stop. How did he respond? *I already know. Do you want to officially meet your daughter? She's in the ranch house, unaware you're her mother.* He had his own secret to tell, but he refused to do anything that would hurt Lexi. What should he do?

"Yell at me. Tell me to go away. Say something." Her voice ended with a squeak.

Satisfied that no one lurked outside, he stuffed his phone in his pocket, lifted his hat and ran a hand over his head. "Your parents have always dictated your life in one way or another. So, I understand your actions—to a point. But why not tell me? We could have worked through it together. Why keep me from my baby?"

"By the time I admitted to myself that I was pregnant, you had already started dating Kaitlyn. My heart shattered. The man I'd loved as a young girl had left me behind. I was alone. Scared of my father's reaction." Her shoulders lifted. "So, I moved and left no forwarding address. I told no one that I was pregnant. I hid my pregnancy by wearing baggy clothes and taking online classes until I delivered our daughter. I never held her." She wrapped her arms across her waist and hunched in on herself. "I knew if I did, I wouldn't let go. I signed the papers, walked out of the hospital and joined the army as soon as I recovered."

His Grace had faced a horrible decision. Her baby or her father's lethal wrath. Cooper had no doubt in his mind that Arthur Harrison would have hurt the infant. The man had emotionally and, now he knew for certain, physically destroyed Grace over the years. Cooper's heart broke for a different reason. Not only for his little girl but also for the young woman who felt she had no choice. But one thing had to be answered before he revealed Lexi's identity. "Do you regret your decision?"

The crease between her brows deepened. "Regret the adoption? No. I would never want a child to endure the evil my father bestowed on me. But not telling you? Yes. The guilt has gnawed at me since the day I walked out of the hospital. I denied you your daughter. For that, I will always live with the guilt and shame."

He considered her response and the why behind it. He might not like it, but he did understand. Now, for the question that would determine his course of action. "If your dear old daddy wasn't part of the equation, would you have kept our daughter?"

Grace's eyes glistened with unshed tears. "My heart aches for the child I'll never know. I didn't want to give her up, but at that moment in my life, I saw no other way to protect her. My father would have fought to possess our child out of spite."

Possess—an accurate description. Cooper strode to the nearest horse's stall and ran his hand over Jasmine's velvet nose. "I have my own secret, Grace. I planned to take it to the grave. I thought that was the right thing to do." His shoulders slumped.

"Whatever it is, it can't be as bad as what I confessed." When he remained silent, she prompted him again. "Cooper?"

God, I don't know if I can do this. What if Lexi gets caught in the middle? His stomach twisted, but God's quiet nudge lightened his heart. Amid all the pain in life, he'd held on to his faith. It's what got him through the tough times. He turned to face Grace. "I've known the truth all along."

She gasped. "How?"

This was it. Time to fess up. He blew out a quick breath. "You put my name on the birth certificate. A social worker called me a few days after you left."

Her hand went to her mouth. "I forgot I did that."

He nodded. "Mrs. Kensley, the social worker, told me about our daughter. She asked if I wanted to sign the adoption paperwork."

A tear trickled down Grace's cheek and dropped from her chin. "You signed the papers."

Here we go. Cooper inhaled a deep breath. "No."

Grace staggered backward. Her eyes widened. "What are you saying?"

"I picked up our baby that day and brought her home." He swallowed the lump crawling up his throat. *Please don't let this be a mistake.* "Lexi is *our* daughter."

A whimper escaped Grace, and her knees buckled.

Cooper hurried to her side and caught her before she hit the ground. He tucked her against his chest and held her as sobs racked her body. He had no idea how long they sat on the dirt floor when her cries turned to sniffs. "I'm sorry."

She gazed up at him with swollen eyes and a red nose. "Why?"

"Why am I sorry?"

She nodded.

"Because I kept our daughter from you. Because I don't know if you ever wanted to find her, and I might have messed that up."

"She... I... Cooper, I shouldn't have withheld the truth from you. I'm the one who's sorry."

"I'm not going to lie. Mrs. Kensley's call shredded me. I was furious with you."

Grace dropped her head, refusing to look at him.

He tucked a finger under her chin and lifted. "But once I held that tiny life in my arms, my anger dissipated."

"I don't know if I'd be as sympathetic."

"Oh, trust me, the hurt lingered, and it didn't take long for my anger to return. Kaitlyn sat me down and asked about your life. Your family. I told her about your parents and the abuse I'd suspected. She forced me to take a step back and look at the big picture. At that point, I might not have liked it, but I understood the why. We decided not to announce Lexi's existence to my mom or the others right away. You know. Work through the abrupt change in our lives first. After about a week of learning the ins and outs of parenting an infant, Kaitlyn agreed to a quick courthouse wedding and stepped into the mom role to help me. She loved Lexi like her own. The family gathering to celebrate our marriage a couple of months or so later was…interesting. My family thought Lexi was Kaitlyn's and mine. They thought she got pregnant while we were dating. We never lied to them. We just didn't correct the assumption." He ran a hand over his hair. "Who am I kidding? It was a lie by omission. But we did it to protect you, Grace."

She placed a hand over her heart. "Me?"

"Yes. I had to talk Kaitlyn out of going to your father and giving him a piece of her mind." He chuckled. His wife had been a feisty one. A woman he grew to love with abandon. "Yeah, in that short time and without knowing you, she became your champion."

"She loved Lexi? Treated her right?"

The question, laced with concern, eased his worries. "More than I can describe. Lexi never wanted for anything, including love." Cooper placed a hand over his chest and pushed against the pain. Losing Kaitlyn had left a void in his life. He'd loved her the best he knew how. Sometimes, it hadn't felt like enough, though. "She never adopted Lexi, but she became her legal guardian."

"She didn't *want* to adopt her?" Grace's wide eyes stared at him.

He shook his head. "It wasn't that. I think she left the door open for you to return. Or maybe she had that deep-down feeling that she wouldn't be around long." Cooper shrugged. "Who knows? But whatever the reason, she did it for you."

Grace pointed to herself. "I didn't deserve that. I walked away and never looked back."

"That may be true, but I don't think you ever stopped loving our baby girl."

Grace hiccuped a sob. "Not once. I tried to forget both of you, but it didn't work."

Cooper couldn't help himself. He pulled her

into a long hug and kissed her forehead. "Now that the truth is no longer a chasm between us, what about Lexi?"

"This is overwhelming. I don't know if I'm ready to tell her yet. I want to get my head on straight first."

The weight pressing down on him lifted. "I'm glad you said that. Lexi is my top priority. She already lost one mother. To discover who you are and you leave would devastate her." Who was he kidding? It would knock him to his knees if Grace walked away.

"I don't plan—"

He held his palm out and tilted his head. "Did you hear that?"

She squinted and listened.

A scratch at the door feathered across the barn.

"Someone's trying to get in the back door. Not the main one. Hide behind the bales of hay and don't move." Cooper reached for his Glock but remembered he'd left it locked in his bedroom gun safe. He'd allowed the ranch to provide a false sense of security. Some FBI agent he was. As quiet as possible, he eased to the back entrance.

The door squeaked open, and Luka stepped inside, almost running into Cooper.

"Hey, man. You startled me."

"What are you doing coming through here?" Cooper pointed to the rarely used door.

Luka grimaced. "I came to check on you."

"And you couldn't use the main entrance?" He flung his hand in the direction of the double door.

"I…uh… I was hoping to catch you alone."

Cooper crossed his arms and stared at his friend. Luka's sneaking around didn't bode well for his innocence. "Why?"

"Luka?" Grace skirted the hay and joined them. "What are you doing here?"

"I came to talk with Cooper, but you know what? It's not important. I'll catch up with you later." Luka spun and marched out of the barn.

Grace watched Luka leave. "That was weird."

Cooper couldn't agree more. "Come on. I don't like how he got in undetected. I need to have a word with the ranch hands. Let's head to the house. We'll figure out how and when to tell Lexi later."

"Sure." Grace shoved her hands in her pockets and strode to the farmhouse, shoulders drooped and head down.

The secrets they'd shared faded into the background. He strode beside her, scanning the yard, his spidey senses on high alert. His mind swirled, attempting to justify Luka's actions.

EIGHT

The headache that had formed last night gripped Grace's temples. She sat on the edge of her bed, tracing the diamond shapes on the colorful quilt with her finger while her mind struggled to grasp her new reality. The truth session between her and Cooper continued to wreak havoc with her brain. He hadn't missed out on his baby's life. The gut-wrenching guilt she'd carried all these years had been unnecessary, but the shame of not telling him remained. No way could she face Lexi, knowing the girl was her daughter. Not yet. How did someone say, *Hi. I'm the woman who never held you and walked away*. Yeah, like that would go over well. If Grace could make her understand the why, Lexi might forgive her. Then again, maybe Grace's insecurities stood in her way. Not Lexi's judgment.

Grace grabbed her jacket and slung her purse over her shoulder, intending to escape the ranch this morning, hoping to avoid Lexi until she wrapped her head around Cooper's earth-shattering news. She tiptoed down the stairs and entered the kitchen on her way to the back door. A lit peppermint candle filled the room with a crisp, intense scent. Soft Christmas music flowed from the smart device on the counter. A reminder of the upcoming holiday. One she hadn't celebrated in years. No, that wasn't right. One she hadn't had others to celebrate with. She adored her employees, but they all had families of their own. If not spouses, parents and siblings. She, on the other hand, had been alone in this world.

"Good morning, Grace."

Of course, she'd run into Mrs. Sinclair before she could escape the ranch. "Morning, Miss Hannah."

"Heading out so soon?" Hannah indicated the bag hanging from Grace's shoulder.

"I…um…have to check in with one of my employees." Not a lie. She did have to meet with Cameron and Laura, but a phone call would suffice.

"Well, then, don't let me keep you, but at least allow me to offer you a cup of coffee before you leave." Hannah poured the brown liquid into a to-go cup and handed it to her.

The bold aroma rose from the small sip hole in the travel mug. "Thank you."

The older woman placed a hand on Grace's arm. "You have always been another one of my children. You know that, right?"

Emotions rolled through her. The woman in front of her—more of a parent than her own. Hannah had shown her what real love was like when she didn't have to. "I appreciate that. I cherished my time with y'all on the ranch."

"Darling, Cooper told me about your father." Hannah tugged her into a hug. "I'm so sorry I didn't see it."

"You weren't supposed to notice. I worked hard to hide it." The times she'd come to the ranch with bruises on her arms, hidden by long-sleeved shirts or the ones on her legs covered by her jeans flitted through her memories. Maybe if she had said something… No. There was no room for second-guessing now. She'd survived. That was the important part.

"I wish you would've told me. I'd have done everything in my power to save you from that pain."

"I know that now. But back then, all I wanted was to avoid my father's anger."

"I get that. But if that man hurts you again, I'm going all Momma Bear on him."

Grace snorted. "I'd pay money to see that."

"It's what we do for those that we love." Hannah squeezed her tighter.

Grace swallowed, fighting tears. "Why didn't my mom protect me?"

"I don't know, sweet girl. But maybe she was a victim of Arthur's wrath too."

She hadn't considered that. Had her father

abused her mother as well? Grace eased from Hannah's embrace. "Thank you." She kissed the older woman on the cheek. "I need to get going. I'm not sure what time I'll be home—I mean back."

The corner of Hannah's mouth lifted. "We'll be waiting for you to come *home* when you finish your work."

Grace nodded and rushed from the house. Between the Lexi news and Hannah's sweet words, she fought the sobs threatening to surface. She fumbled the car keys as she tried to push the button to unlock her SUV.

"Gracie, wait up." Cooper hurried toward her, hobbling a bit from his recent injuries.

"I'm sorry. I have to go." She couldn't handle speaking with him or anyone else right now. The lock clicked. She flung the door open and slid behind the steering wheel.

"Please, wait." Cooper placed his hands on the roof of her vehicle and peered into the driver's side. "I don't like you going off by yourself. If you give me about twenty minutes, I'll come with you."

"No."

Cooper jerked like she'd slapped him.

She softened her tone. "I need time to myself after our confession session last night. It's a lot to process. I'll be careful."

He covered his mouth and slid his hand down over his chin. "I guess I've known the truth for eight years. You were blindsided by it last night. But promise me you won't interview or investigate anyone alone."

"That I can do. I won't be stupid." With a killer on the loose, she'd be hyperaware of her surroundings and call for help the minute she became uncomfortable. But she refused to allow her attacker to control her actions. Her father had done that for far too long. It was time to take her life back.

"That's all I can ask. Go. Process that your daughter is asleep in there." He pointed to the ranch house behind him. "But please, whatever you do, don't tell her. Not yet."

Tears filled her eyes. "I won't." She started the engine and drove off down the lane away from the man who had turned her world upside down.

She gave a quick look into the rearview mirror—Cooper stood motionless, head down, hands in his pocket. Dejected? Maybe. Concerned? Most definitely. Between her watery vision and the harsh glow of the sunrise reflection on the windshield, Grace flipped down the visor and slipped on her sunglasses. Wet trails streaked down her cheeks and dropped into her lap.

The past—a quagmire of emotions. Grace had no idea what Lexi looked like as a baby since she'd chosen not to hold her after giving birth. What kind of toddler had she been? Timid like Grace or vivacious like her father? A vise constricted her chest, forcing the air from her lungs.

She gasped for air like a fish flopping on the riverbank. She desperately wanted to hold Lexi in her arms. But her father remained in the picture, and she refused to allow him to taint Lexi's life.

She aimed her SUV toward the rodeo grounds. The early morning meant few people were up and around, leaving Grace to soak up the peace in the place that had given her comfort over the years.

The parking lot near the barn was empty. The rodeo participants who lived in campers parked on the far end at the request of the rodeo director. She'd have the area to herself, at least for the next hour or so. As she eased her way through the lot, the gravel popping under her tires, she scanned the grounds. She had no intention of ignoring the threat to her life.

Her vehicle in Park and the door locks checked, Grace toyed with her phone. To call Cameron and Laura or sit and watch the remainder of the sunrise? Her phone buzzed. She glanced at the caller ID and smiled. The decision made for her, she hit Accept. "Good morning, Cameron." Resting against the headrest, she closed her eyes.

"Good morning to you too, boss lady."

"How many times have I told you to stop calling me that?"

"Blah, blah, blah. Whatever." Her employee laughed. "Do you want to argue, or do you want to hear what I found?"

Grace sighed. The man was the best business

manager she could ask for, but sometimes he drove her bananas. "Please tell me you found something good."

"Meh, that's debatable, but it's worth discussing."

"Then quit keeping me in suspense." The banter between the two of them settled her spinning mind. Her usual routine with a job she loved. A week ago, her life made sense. Now? Not so much.

"Fine. I tracked down the bull rider Barry's girlfriend. Or should I say I found her information."

Grace sat up and gripped the steering wheel. "Did you talk with her? Find out whether or not she knew if Barry had heart problems that he didn't disclose to the rodeo doctors?"

"That's just it. Thanks to social media, I have her name and picture, but it's like she vanished into thin air. I can't find her."

She slumped in her seat at the news. "Could she be a victim of our killer? You know, she saw too much, and he eliminated her?"

"I don't like the way you think."

She huffed out a humorless laugh. "Neither do I, but I had to ask."

Cameron sighed. "It's a possibility, but nothing leads me to that conclusion except for her lack of visibility after Barry's death."

"Text me her name and photo. I'll see if I recognize her." She palmed her phone and waited.

"Hang on." Cameron's text came through a minute later.

She studied the image. "Sydney Zorn. I can't say I know her. She looks a bit familiar, though, but I don't know why."

"Barry died before the rodeo director hired you. I doubt she hung around after her boyfriend's heart attack since she didn't participate in the rodeos. There's no reason you should recognize her. Then again, from what I've uncovered, she's a buckle bunny."

Grace laughed. "Look at you using the lingo."

"Very funny. Not much difference between that and badge bunnies." Cameron sighed. "I don't get it. Women going after cowboys, police officers or firefighters just because of the buckle or badge." Cameron was handsome and had retired from a career in law enforcement, so she suspected he'd dealt with his fair share of these types of women.

"I don't get it either." She rubbed her temples. "Keep looking for Ms. Zorn. I'd like to chat with her."

"Will do." The tapping of keys popped in the background. "I took the liberty of setting up an interview with Bateman's girlfriend, Macey Webster. She'll meet you outside the rodeo barn in about an hour."

She gazed at the sun now sitting well above the horizon. Movement at the far end of the parking lot signaled the start of the day. Cowboys and cowgirls stirred but were not quite up and ready to begin their routines of taking care of the animals. "Not a problem."

"I know you can handle yourself, but please let Laura or myself join you. I don't trust what's going on at the rodeo grounds."

"Keep working on background checks and finding the missing girlfriend. I'll call Cooper. If I don't include him, he'll get all growly."

Cameron chuckled. "I like this guy already. I have to meet him in person."

"And someday you will. Go. Get to work."

"Yes, ma'am." He hung up before she could scold him for calling her ma'am.

Due to the early hour and the fact she hadn't updated Donovan Keats with the latest information, instead of calling, she typed a text message with the basics and hit Send. She hadn't wanted to cross the line and disclose what might be considered part of the sheriff's department investigation, but the man who hired her deserved to be kept up to date.

With her report sent, Grace slipped from her SUV. Fists in her lower back, she arched, stretching the muscles that had stiffened from her latest adventures. She snorted. *Adventures. Yeah, let's go with that.* She zipped her jacket. The warmth of the fleece—instantaneous. The calves bawling in the distance mingled with the huffs and whinnies of the horses, waking for the day.

A deep inhalation of the cool morning air eased her battered nerves. Keeping her word to Cooper, she shot off a text.

Grace: Interview with Macey @ 7:30 in the rodeo barn.

Cooper: I'll be there.

Grace: Figured.

Cooper: I'm serious, Gracie. Wait for me.

She rolled her eyes. Had everyone assumed she'd lost her mind?

Grace: I'm not stupid.

Cooper: Never said you were.

She started to tuck her phone away when the bubble of dots appeared.

Cooper: We need to talk after the interview.

Of course, he wanted to discuss last night. She just wasn't sure she had it in her. Her brain struggled to process the new reality.

Grace: Maybe.

She shoved the device into her pocket, leaned against her SUV and allowed the sun to shine on her face. A few minutes later, she strode toward the horse barn. A little equine therapy was in order. The door squeaked open, and she stepped inside. A smile tugged on her lips. This—this was her happy place. As much as her mind tried to hold on to the anger that her parents, mainly her father, had pushed her away from her hometown and friends, from a part-time job of bullfighting that she loved, the comforting smell of hay and horse filled her heart, chasing away the resentment, at least for the moment.

"Hey, boy. How are you?" Grace approached a beautiful tan quarter horse and ran her fingers from his forehead to his velvet nose. "You like that, don't you."

The horse's head bobbed up and down.

With each hand stroke on the horse's nose, her worries and insecurities melted away. She knew it would be temporary, but for now, she'd bask in the calmness.

A commotion sounded at the far end of the barn in the pen that held the steers.

She squinted in the direction of the odd stirring of hoofed animals. "I'll be back, boy." Her boots clomped along the pathway between the stalls. The echo thudded in her chest. What had riled the steers? She slowed, approaching the pen with caution. "What's going on in there?" she asked the animals in a soft tone. "Did something bother you?"

Grace scanned the enclosure. Nothing seemed out of place and the steers had calmed. Strange. She spun at the thunk to her right and squinted into the shadows.

A sharp pain jabbed her neck. She swatted away the offending object. Her gaze locked onto a dart lying in the dirt at her feet. The world whirled. She dropped to the ground, straining to see through the collapsing tunnel. She had to call Cooper for help, but her limbs refused to move.

Hands scooped under her arms and lifted. Her legs scraped along the dirt. A latch clicked, and she flopped to the ground. Her body twisted, and her jacket disappeared. The cold made her shiver, and the odor of manure filled her nose. Hooves stomped close by. Her muddled mind clued in. Someone had thrown her into the pen of steers with no protection. Not even her coat. Not that it would have done much.

She fought her jumbled thoughts. She had to move. If any of the steers' hooves stomped on her head, she'd be dead.

Her mind snapped to Lexi, the precious girl she had an opportunity to reconnect with after eight years. She had to survive. For her daughter and Cooper, the man she'd lost and found again.

God, please don't let me die. She hoped He listened to her, and she had the opportunity to right the wrongs of her life.

She fought the losing battle of consciousness. The abyss yanked her to its depths.

Cooper had spent the last half an hour talking himself out of rushing to Grace's side. As he'd grabbed his keys and headed for the back door, his mother trapped him in the house discussing Christmas. Whether unintentional or on purpose, he wasn't sure. Hannah Sinclair had a knack for recognizing what her children needed. Apparently, she'd determined he should give Grace space. So, he sat and listened—until he couldn't. When the worry gnawed a hole in his stomach, he kissed his mom on the cheek, apologized for leaving and hurried out the door. Once in his truck, he drove as fast as possible without getting a ticket to the rodeo grounds.

He entered the parking lot and spotted Grace's SUV. The unease that had struck several minutes ago increased. He parked next to her vehicle and dropped from his rental truck.

"Grace?" He peered into the SUV. Nothing. He spun in a slow circle. Where had the woman gone? He tapped a fisted hand to his forehead. "Come on, Cooper. Think." The horses! He jogged to the barn and slipped inside. "Gracie?"

Pop! Pop! Pop!

Firecrackers exploded from where they kept

the steers. Cooper sprinted down the middle aisle of the barn toward the ruckus. He skidded to a stop. It took a second for his mind to catch up to the horror before him.

Grace lay on the ground in the pen, steers running in panic inside the enclosure.

"Gracie!"

He vaulted over the fence and waved his arms. "Yaah! Get back!" He spun and scooped Grace up and busted through the gate. A quick hip check closed it behind him. He cradled her and carried her farther into the barn. Once inside, he slid to the ground using the wall as a backrest. "Gracie, honey? Wake up and let me see those beautiful blue eyes."

"Mr. Sinclair?"

He jerked his gaze to the blonde standing a few feet away. "Macey?"

She nodded. "I heard the firecrackers and the commotion and came running. Is there anything I can do?"

"Did you see anything? Hear anything? What are you doing here?" The rapid-fire questions weren't helping, but Cooper's brain had short-circuited when he'd seen the steers' hooves too close to Grace's head.

Macey wrapped her arms around her waist and jutted her chin toward Grace. "I had a meeting with her. I got here a few minutes early."

Oh, yeah. The interview had slipped Cooper's

mind. "Sorry. I'm a bit… Sorry. Could you call 9-1-1 and request an ambulance?" He refocused on the woman in his arms. "Gracie, please wake up." He tuned out the woman's conversation with the dispatcher and brushed Gracie's cheek with the back of his hand.

"I think I found something." Macey held up a metal object.

"That looks like a tranquilizer dart." His veterinarian sister kept them in her kit in case one of the animals got out of hand. "Where did you find it?"

Macey pivoted and pointed toward the pen gate. "I was pacing while on the phone and spotted it over there."

"Bring it here. I'll give it to the sheriff when she shows up." Wait. He hadn't called his sister.

Bateman's girlfriend handed him the dart. He accepted the offending object, held it so he wouldn't destroy any remaining evidence and placed it on the ground beside his leg. He'd have Izzie run it for fingerprints, but more than likely, Macey had smudged any viable prints when she handled it. And, of course, he added to it by not wearing gloves.

Heart still pounding from how he discovered Grace, he wiggled the phone from his pocket and hit Izzie's speed dial number.

"Hey, Coop, that was a fast interview."

"Didn't happen." He glanced at Macey and then

back to Grace. "I need you at the steer pen on the rodeo grounds as fast as you can get here."

"On my way. Stay on the line." Cooper heard her running footsteps and her car door slam shut. "Now, tell me what happened."

He rested his head against the barn wall and closed his eyes, aware that Macey continued to watch him. "As you know, I came to meet up with Grace. When I got here, I couldn't find her, then I heard firecrackers."

"Whoa, what?"

"You heard me. I ran to the steer pen and found Grace unconscious on the ground inside. I jumped in, grabbed her and raced out before we got trampled." He hesitated, unsure if he'd said too much in front of Macey. Although, she *had* found the dart.

"Coop?"

"Sorry, what?"

"If she didn't get stepped on, why isn't Grace awake?"

"I'm making an assumption here, based on evidence found. Someone tagged her with a tranquilizer dart."

"Ambulance?"

"Called."

"Any witnesses?"

"Uncertain. Grace had a meeting scheduled with Macey Webster. Macey showed up after I rescued Grace. She's the one who found the dart."

Izzie released an audible huff. "I know you're concentrating on Grace, but don't let anyone stomp all over my crime scene."

"You mean besides Grace, Macey and myself when I saved her? Oh, yeah, don't forget the steers." He should tone down his attitude, but at the moment he didn't care.

"Yeah, yeah, I get the picture. By the way, sarcasm doesn't become you."

"Give me a break on this one, will ya?" Cooper clenched his teeth. His Gracie remained motionless. He sucked in a breath—*his* Gracie. Yes, she had been his since the first time they'd met. Then, life had separated them.

"Since it's Grace, you know I will."

"Thanks, sis. I hear the ambulance siren now." The air-piercing sound sent relief shooting through him.

"Good. I'm about ten minutes out. I'll talk with you in a bit." Izzie disconnected.

He hadn't realized what a lifeline his sister had become until she hung up. Cooper curled Grace into him and kissed the top of her head. How had he ever walked away from her? It appeared that shame and guilt had marred their paths. Why had he let the town's image of him get in the way of what he'd always wanted? Grace. The town was wrong, by the way. He'd never been a player like his old man. He'd experienced the devastation

Wayne Sinclair had left in his wake with affair after affair.

"Gracie?" He smoothed the hair from her face and tucked a wayward strand of a blond curl behind her ear. "I'm sorry for so many things."

"What do we have, Cooper?"

He glanced up. Paramedic Noah strode toward him, with his partner Harper in his wake. "Based on evidence, a tranquilizer dart. I found her in the steer pen. The animals were going crazy. They might have stepped on her."

"I'll get the gurney." Harper spun and jogged off.

Noah crouched next to him. "Coop, I need to take a look."

"Yeah, right. Sure." What was wrong with him? His entire experience as an FBI agent had flown the chicken coop when he'd spotted Grace inside the pen with the terrified animals. He loosened his grip and laid her on the ground but sat in a straddle, keeping her head and shoulders propped on his chest.

Noah took her pulse and listened to her lungs. After a quick assessment, he removed the stethoscope from his ears and flipped it around his neck. "From what I can tell, she's asleep. I don't see any major injuries. She has a scrape on her arm. I'm guessing a hoof caught her there, but nothing serious."

Harper approached with the gurney. She and

Noah got to work moving Grace onto the rolling bed.

Cooper struggled to his feet. His stomach whirled like when he rode the scrambler at the carnival too many times. He could have found the woman he'd loved since his teenage years trampled beneath the hooves of several dozen steers, weighing up to a thousand pounds. He swallowed the bile creeping up his throat.

"Cooper!" Izzie strode toward him and engulfed him in a hug.

"Izzie." He closed his eyes and absorbed his sister's comfort. "She seems okay, just asleep."

"Good." His sister released him. "I'll get my deputies to canvass the area and process the scene. Go with her to the hospital. I'll have your truck delivered later."

He studied his sister for a moment, then handed her his keys. "I'll keep you posted on her condition."

"I'd appreciate that. I'll need your statement and hers when she wakes up, but for now, go with Noah and Harper. Take care of your girl."

His girl? Yeah, she'd been his girl for as long as he could remember. He snorted.

Izzie's brow arched.

He shook his head and waved off her question. "The dart is over there. Let me know what you find."

"I've got this. Go." Izzie spun and barked orders at her deputies.

Cooper jogged behind the gurney. "Noah, I'm going with her."

"We assumed." Harper threw the comment over her shoulder.

He jumped into the back of the ambulance, sat on the bench and threaded his fingers with hers.

Harper clutched her stethoscope in her hand. "Her vitals are good. From what you told us about the sedative, I'm guessing she'll be out for a while. But the docs will do blood tests to confirm the drug and possible side effects."

The lump inhabiting his throat blocked a response, so he nodded. Cooper bowed his head. *God, please protect her. Help her fight off whatever this drug is. I need her in my life.* Keeping his faith strong and intact had gotten him through the tough times in life. God had never failed him. Oh sure, Cooper might have wanted different outcomes, but he trusted God. The Big Guy had never let him down.

Chaos ensued when they parked at the emergency department doors. The paramedics and nurses whisked Grace away, leaving him standing at the entrance. Unsure what to do next, he moved to the reception counter.

"Hey, Cooper, how are you holding up?" The lady working at the desk and his mother had a friendship that dated back to their childhood. The woman was family.

"Hi, Aunt Rachel. I'm okay, I suppose."

"So, not good."

He gave a humorless laugh. "You know me well." Cooper ran a hand along his nape. "Are the HIPAA documents the same as before?"

Rachel nodded. "You have privileges."

"And her parents?"

"Are not to be told anything about her condition or allowed to see her without her or your permission."

He lifted his eyes to the ceiling. *Thank you, God.* One less thing to worry about. Arthur's perceived perfect reputation would come into play, and someone would express their concern, inadvertently telling him about Grace's incident. He would show up, and there was no doubt in Cooper's mind Arthur Harrison would cause a ruckus. It helped to know Cooper had the authority to keep him away from Grace. "Let me know as soon as you hear anything?"

"You know I will. Go sit. It'll be a while."

Cooper rapped his knuckles on the desk, then ambled into the waiting room. The cheery Christmas tree in the corner of the room and the twinkling lights around the window did nothing for his mental state. Not even the three-foot stuffed dog with a Santa hat could make him smile. He plopped onto a chair. Exhaustion pulled at him, making him feel ten years older. Elbows on his knees, he buried his face in his hands and waited for news.

"Cooper."

He lifted his head, searching for who'd called his name.

Izzie strode in and sat next to him. She wrapped her arms around him and held on.

The comfort of his sister's embrace released the tears he'd held at bay when he'd rescued Grace from being trampled.

"Oh, Coop. I'm so sorry. I'm failing miserably with this case, and it's put you and Grace in danger."

He swiped tears from his cheeks and cupped her face. "Don't. This isn't your fault. It's as much my case as it is yours. We've missed something. And that stops now. Once she's awake and discharged, we're reviewing everything we have. That includes what her employees have dug up as well. Anyone and everything attached to this case."

"Agreed. We'll meet at the sheriff's department office. I need your statements, and after that, I'll commandeer the conference room. This has to end now."

"I should have known." Arthur Harrison paused at the entrance of the waiting room. He straightened his suit coat and lifted his chin.

Cooper shot to his feet. The man's arrogant

stance made Cooper want to slug him. Especially now that Grace had confessed what the man had done to her as a teen. "And like last time, you aren't welcome."

"We'll see about that." Arthur strode to the desk. "I'd like information on *my daughter*'s condition."

Cooper and Izzie joined the jerk.

"I'm sorry, Mr. Harrison. You are not on Grace's HIPAA list, and before you ask, you are not allowed to see her either."

"By whose authority?" Arthur's voice skyrocketed, causing people to stare.

Cooper widened his stance and crossed his arms. "That would be mine." He noticed a doctor motion him over.

"You have no—"

He lifted his hand, palm up. "Hold that thought." As he met the doctor at the double doors leading to the emergency bays, Izzie blocked Harrison's path. Cooper dropped his voice low so Grace's father couldn't hear. "How is she?"

"Groggy. But she'll be fine once the drugs wear off."

"Can I see her?"

"Of course." The doctor jutted his chin toward Arthur. "I've been informed of the situation and the previous orders. Plus, Grace woke up enough to state that you have the authority for all her medical and personal decisions. That man will not be given information or have access to her unless you say otherwise."

"Thank you." Cooper released a long, slow breath.

"If you'll follow me." The doctor placed a hand on the door.

"Just a second." Cooper's gaze connected with his sister's. "Izzie?"

She waved him off. "I've got this."

He nodded, happy to leave Arthur behind in his sister's capable hands. "Let's go, Doc."

A few moments later, he entered the semi-private bay and got his first look at Grace. He sucked in an audible breath.

"She'll be fine once the drug wears off."

"She doesn't look okay." His heart rate increased at her stillness under the white blanket tucked around her.

The doctor smiled. "Go sit with her. You'll feel better the next time she wakes up." The man patted him on the back and left Cooper staring at the woman who'd stolen his heart.

Cooper walked over and sat on a hard plastic chair next to Grace's bed. He laced his fingers with hers. "Gracie?"

Her eyelids fluttered.

Relief washed over him. "Come on, I need to see that you're okay with my own eyes."

Slowly, her eyes opened. "Cooper?"

"Yeah, honey, it's me."

"I feel like I got run over by a bull."

He chuckled. "Not quite, but close."

Her eyes shot open, and she grimaced. "What?"

"Easy there." He rubbed small circles on the back of her hand with his thumb. "You don't remember?"

"Apparently not." She lifted her free hand to her forehead. "The headache's a bear. Kinda feels like that time when I was fifteen, and I hit my head on the wall."

He didn't remember that, but he'd discovered, even as close as they'd been, he didn't know as much about her childhood as he'd thought. "Can't say I recall that."

"Oh, well, I…" She sucked in a breath and winced. "Tell me what happened."

Her reluctance to spill the story had him wondering if the injury had something to do with her father—again. But he wouldn't press. "Sure. I can only tell you what happened after arriving at the rodeo grounds. You'll have to wait for the fog to lift to get the whole story from your memories."

For the next few minutes, he told her what he knew for a fact and threw in a few assumptions along the way.

"How did I become a target? Why is someone determined to kill me?" A tear trickled from the corner of her eye.

Cooper caught the droplet before it made its

way into her ear. "I don't know, Gracie, but I intend to find out and eliminate the problem."

He hadn't meant he'd kill the person. He was law enforcement and relied on justice. Unless he had no choice in order to save her life.

NINE

The fluorescent lights in the sheriff's office conference room mixed with the natural light from the partially closed blinds on the window made Grace's headache worse by the minute. Since her memory had returned, she'd given her statement to one of the deputies, called Keats with another update and assured him her injuries weren't serious, then insisted on joining Cooper, Izzie and Daniel to review the case. But after thirty minutes of being in the room, she regretted her determination to push through the discomfort.

Cooper tugged his sunglasses from where he'd slipped them on the front of his black long-sleeve T-shirt and placed them on her face. "There. That should help."

She turned his gaze to him. "How'd you know?"

He pulled the glasses down and ran a finger between her eyes. "I remember how the crease here deepens when you have a headache."

It amazed her how Cooper read her so well. She had perfected the art of concealment during her youth, but not with him. "Thank you." She pushed the sunglasses up. They had an immediate effect. "The lights in here are not great for my head."

"I assumed. You've been squinting since the doc discharged you a couple of hours ago."

She ignored his unspoken statement that she should have stayed overnight and not left the hospital.

Izzie strode in, saving Grace from having to defend her decision. "Where's Daniel?"

"I'm here." Daniel sauntered in, plopped onto a chair and grinned. "Couldn't live without me?"

"Oh, please." Izzie rolled her eyes. "Why did I hire you?"

"Because you love me, sis." He waggled his eyebrows. Classic class clown.

Grace struggled to keep the smile from forming, but it didn't work. Daniel never failed to ease tension with his goofy ways. In and out of the rodeo arena. One of the many reasons she enjoyed working with him. But it was the brother beside her that held her heart—always had. The town that had made him out to be the bad boy didn't know him at all. And how had that reputation started? She hadn't a clue.

Cooper leaned in and whispered, "You're thinking too hard."

About you. "Sorry."

"No need to be sorry." He clasped her hand and squeezed.

She expected him to let go, but he maintained his soft grip.

Izzie set her cup of coffee down and took a seat at the head of the table. "Are your employees coming?" She directed her question at Grace.

"Cameron is working on information from the first deaths and won't be here in person, but he said he's happy to join a conference call. Laura plans to join us." Grace glanced at her watch. "She should be here any minute."

As if on cue, Laura poked her head into the room. When her gaze landed on Grace, relief washed over her face. "Oh good, I'm in the right place."

"Come on in." Grace gestured to an empty seat. "Everyone, I'd like you to meet one of my best investigators, Laura. Laura, this is Cooper, Sheriff Sinclair, aka Izzie, and Daniel."

Laura collapsed onto a chair next to Daniel. She dropped her bag to the floor and placed the laptop she'd hugged when entering onto the table. "Nice to meet you all." She ran her fingers through her disheveled hair. The dark circles rimming her eyes stood out like a New York businessman in dirty cowboy boots.

The woman was a hot mess on a good day, but somehow, she rocked the private investigator gig. "Have you been up all night?" Grace pointed the question at her employee and friend.

Laura held up her finger and thumb an inch apart. "Maybe a little bit."

Daniel arched a brow. "That doesn't even make sense."

"Meh." Laura shrugged. "Anyhoos, what did I miss?" She scanned the group. "I usually miss something."

The group of siblings' gazes connected with each other, and they had a silent conversation among themselves.

Grace chuckled. "I promise she's great at her job."

Daniel studied Laura for a moment. "Let's see what you've got, sweetheart."

"Watch it, buster." Laura glared at him.

Oh boy, here we go. "Don't start, you two." Grace rubbed her temples.

"What?" Daniel spread his arms, palms up.

"Behave, bro." Cooper placed his hand on her arm and rubbed circles on the inside of her wrist. The motion, calming and full of unspoken words. "If y'all are done messing around, I'd like to get down to business."

Daniel's gaze shifted to her. "Sorry, Grace."

She gave him a half smile, then faced Izzie, waiting for her friend to take control of the meeting. An odd feeling since she owned GracePoint Security, and that was typically her job. But under the circumstances, she'd happily hand over the reins to Izzie.

"Get Cameron on the phone. I want a rundown of the information everyone has."

"I'll call him." Laura started dialing before Izzie finished her request.

"Perfect. Daniel, once he's on the line, I want to hear what you learned about Luka." Izzie grabbed a pad of paper and a pen.

Laura placed her phone on speaker. "Cameron's on."

"Thanks for joining us." Izzie tapped her pen on the table.

"Anything for Grace." Laura nodded in agreement to Cameron's declaration.

"Let's get started. Daniel, you're up."

Daniel leaned his forearms on the table. "After talking with Chris and getting the general lowdown on the bull riders, I decided to be upfront with Luka, at least to a point. I told him about someone tampering with the rope. The man turned six shades of Casper white. Then I brought up the missing phone and the text messages. If a hay bale hadn't caught his fall, the man's tuchus would have ended up on the ground. No one is that good of an actor."

"Are you saying he's not a suspect?" The hopeful tone in Cooper's question twisted Grace's insides.

"My initial gut reaction? No, he's not responsible for your fall or Grace getting locked in that camper. But doing my due diligence, I dug into

Luka's background. He's ridden in a lot of rodeos over the season, but not all of them. I asked a few questions around the rodeo family and used my supersleuth skills. The man has a side job, and you're not going to believe what it is." Daniel paused and checked his fingernails, leaving them in suspense.

Izzie leaned forward. Her eyebrows raised. "Spit it out, D."

He grinned at Cooper. "You can relax, bro. Luka isn't responsible. The man is ATF."

"He's an agent with the Bureau of Alcohol, Tobacco, Firearms and Explosives?" Cooper's wide-eyed gaze scanned those sitting around the table. "How did I not know that?"

"Government work at its finest. Plus, remember, I brought the FBI in on a hunch. No one knows why you're here either." Izzie rubbed her eyes. "And if Luka thought you'd given up on the FBI, he'd hesitate to tell you anything."

"So, when he showed up at the ranch, he hadn't come for nefarious reasons." Cooper's shoulders drooped in relief.

Grace gripped his fingers. "I'm making an assumption here. But I'm wondering if, after speaking with Daniel, he took it upon himself to watch out for us and got caught because of the squeaky door. Maybe he planned to let you in on his undercover assignment."

"That makes as much sense as anything else," Daniel agreed.

"I'll chat with his supervisor before I open up to Luka. Just in case." Izzie jotted down a note.

"I'll go next." Laura undid her messy bun and redid it. The result didn't help neaten the woman's hair, but Grace knew her employee's nervous habit.

Izzie motioned for her to continue.

"I made contact with Billy." Laura winked at Grace.

Oh, that girl. She had a way of blending in or sticking out, whichever the case required. And she wasn't shy about it.

"After a bit of encouragement, he fessed up to sabotaging Cooper's ride. Although he's adamant that he hadn't tried to kill him. Just cause him not to ride the whole eight seconds and get him knocked out of the finals, making it easier for Billy to win the purse money. After spending time with him, I believe him. He's greedy and full of himself. Not a killer."

Daniel scowled at Laura. "Did you flirt with him?"

"Oh, relax. We had a nice conversation." Laura rolled her eyes.

Grace inhaled and winced at the aches and pains her body had endured over the past few days. "We've crossed Luka and Billy off the killer list. Cooper and I never interviewed Bateman's girlfriend, Macey Webster, so that's an unknown for now. Before I became a pincushion and ragdoll for the steers, Cameron mentioned an insurance policy for one of the other bull riders who died."

Cameron latched on to the opportunity. "After calling in a few favors, I discovered that Barry Larsen's girlfriend, Sydney Zorn, was his fiancée. She received a two-million-dollar life insurance policy payout when the coroner ruled his death a heart attack, which wasn't a stretch since he had a family history of heart disease. No one questioned it. And honestly, why should they?"

"Barry's death seems on the up and up. So, we cross him off the murdered list then?" Daniel asked.

"Not so fast." Izzie pointed to herself. "I had the coroner take a second look at his records and lab results with a suspicious eye. He found an anomaly with the blood tests. He reran it."

"Again? How'd he do that?" Laura asked.

"He keeps blood samples for a designated amount of time after the autopsies. Anyway—" Izzie flicked her hand as if brushing off the detour of conversation "—he called me this morning with the new results. He found minute traces of succinylcholine. If he hadn't looked for it, he said he never would have discovered it."

"So, definitely murder."

Izzie nodded.

Cooper flipped through the file in front of him. "And what about Ryan Brown?"

"I'll take that one." Cameron spoke up from the speaker on the table. "The police department in Coyote Bluff, Texas, where his accident happened, stated the truck had extensive damage. However, one of the good ol' boy mechanics in town told me he couldn't prove it but thought the brake line had been tampered with."

Grace shifted in her chair, relieving the pressure on her bruises. "Did he give you specifics?"

"No. When the guy realized he said too much, he clammed up."

"Nice work, Cameron."

"Awe, boss, you're making me blush."

Grace rolled her eyes. "Between you and Daniel, I'm surrounded by class clowns."

Daniel slapped a hand over his heart. "I'm offended."

"Sure you are, bro." Cooper narrowed his gaze at his brother. "Can we get on with this? Someone is trying to kill Gracie."

She gripped his forearm. "It's okay. We all need a bit of levity right now."

"Sorry." The crease on his forehead deepened. "I just want the threat against you stopped."

"Wait a second." Laura held up a hand, then continued to type. "I have an email from my go-to information guy. It appears Bateman had a two-million-dollar insurance policy as well."

"Let me guess—Miss Macey Webster is the beneficiary." Daniel leaned back and clasped his hands over his chest.

Laura shook her head but never lost focus on her laptop screen. "Nope."

Daniel pitched forward. "Say what now?"

"The money went to Wrangler's Way Ventures, Bateman's silent sponsor. The weird thing is that I can't find anything on the company. As in no website or mention of the business online."

"That's odd." Grace racked her brain to come up with a reason her employee couldn't get a hit on the company. "A shell corporation, maybe?"

"Possibly." Izzie lifted the conference room phone and asked one of her deputies to look into the policy and the invisible company. "As soon as Brian gets me that information, I want someone talking to the insurance agent who wrote the policy."

Cooper raised a finger. "Depending on where it is, Grace and I will take that. Afterward, we'll interview Macey. See if Bateman told her anything about his policy or his sponsor."

"The interviews are yours. Laura, do a deep dive and see if there's an insurance policy we missed on Ryan Brown."

"You got it."

"I'm calling the sheriffs in the respective counties to take a second look into Lance's hunting accident and Brent's overdose. Those deaths don't sit well with me. I'll have them check insurance payouts too." Izzie jotted down more notes. "Any other possible suspects or elimination of suspects?" Izzie met each person's gaze. "No? Okay. Anything else that we should discuss?"

Cooper turned to face Grace. His eyes widened, and his teeth clenched.

"What is it?" she asked, unsure she wanted to know.

"Laura, Cameron, I think we've covered it all for now. Please let us know what else you discover." The FBI agent in Cooper surfaced.

"Will do. I'm out." Cameron hung up.

Laura scanned the conference room. "Okay, then. I guess I'm out of here too." Her gaze connected with Grace's. "Call me if you need anything." With that, Laura gathered her laptop and bag and escaped the growing tension.

"Coop?" Daniel stared at his brother.

Cooper stood and paced the room. "What if…" He whipped around and met her eyes. "Your father."

She sucked in a breath. "No. I mean, yes, he did… But not this. I can't…" According to Cooper, Arthur had shown up to the hospital twice and once at the rodeo. However, threatening her in public? She couldn't see it. But then again…

"Want to share with the class?" Daniel asked.

Izzie tapped her lip with her pen and arched an eyebrow.

Cooper sat on the edge of his chair and scooped her hand into his. "It's time to tell them. Even if I'm wrong about this."

Grace fought her fears and shame. Daniel and Izzie deserved to know. They'd been friends for years. More like siblings. "Okay." Her voice chose that moment not to work, so the word came out as a whisper.

The pair of siblings glanced from her to Cooper and back. She'd laugh at their expressions if the truth wasn't so depressing. "I'm sure you can guess that my childhood had its challenges."

"I'd say so. Your father's attitude toward you rivaled a branding iron. Leaving marks that are impossible to erase." Daniel's snarled words shocked her. The man had easygoing down to a science.

"It's taken me years to shake the fear and build my confidence." She exhaled. "Y'all knew my father was emotionally abusive. But what I hid from you was the physical abuse."

A collective gasp filled the otherwise silent room.

The muscles in Cooper's neck and shoulders tightened. Guilt from his lack of awareness oozed from him. But he had nothing to blame himself for. He'd been her rock. The person she went to for strength.

She proceeded to fill in the blanks of her story—her childhood reality.

When she finished, tears dripped from Izzie's chin. "I should have been a better friend."

"No. Please don't say that. I hid my family life from you—my shame. When I came to the ranch, I wanted to feel normal. Y'all gave me that. A sense of real family." A tear leaked from the corner of Grace's eye. "That's why I haven't returned to Rollins. I had to stay away from my father."

Daniel ran a hand over his head, messing up his hair. "I wish you would have said something."

"I went away to college and then joined the army. More to escape my problems than to fulfill a dream. But the military taught me confidence. I served my years, then moved to Lackard and opened GracePoint Security. I've worked hard and created a successful business. It's amazing how being out from under dear ol' dad's control gave me the strength to be me."

"Did Coop know?" Daniel asked.

"Of course not." Cooper bellowed at his brother. "I just found out."

"Relax, man, I was only asking. I'm not accusing you."

Cooper stood and paced the room like he had earlier. He spun and looked out the window. "What is he doing here!" He bolted out of the conference room. The door slammed behind him.

"Cooper?" Grace hurried to the window. "Oh, no."

"Who is it?" Izzie asked.

She turned and faced Daniel and Izzie. "My father."

Grace sprinted out the door, chasing Cooper before he did something that landed him in trouble.

How dare Arthur Harrison show his face anywhere near Grace after how he'd treated her. The man deserved to go to prison for his actions. Cooper's anger was held at bay by the thinnest of threads. He pushed through the sheriff's department front doors and stalked toward the man. His molars clenched tight, and his hands fisted. The crisp December air did little to cool his temper.

"I suggest you leave. Now!" Cooper stopped a few feet from the despicable man.

Arthur grinned and held his arms out. "I have every right to be here. I'm checking on my daughter like any good parent would."

"You're a sorry excuse for a father." Cooper leaned in, keeping his voice low. "She told me what you've done."

A flicker of disbelief flashed across Arthur's face and vanished. "That girl has a wild imagination and is a disgrace to the family name. No one will believe a word she says. Not since she hung out with a delinquent like you."

No one had thought less of him until the summer when his relationship with Grace had grown beyond simple friendship. He hadn't done anything to deserve the reputation. The truth sucker punched him in the gut. Cooper snatched the front of the man's shirt, the material in his fists. "It was you, wasn't it? I never understood why people turned on me, labeling me the town's bad boy. I worked hard at school and on the ranch. In the little spare time I had, I rode in the regional rodeos. I rarely dated before the rumor. I had done nothing to warrant the player reputation." He tightened his grip. "You started the rumors, didn't you?"

"Apple. Tree." Arthur bobbed his hands up and down like weighing his words on a scale.

"Cooper, let go of him." Izzie's sheriff's voice rang out.

A petite hand he'd recognize anywhere rested on his bicep. "Please come back inside. He's not worth it."

He barely heard Grace over the blood whooshing in his ears.

"Well, hello, Grace. How's my little girl?" The sickening, sweet words dripped from Arthur's tongue.

She glared at her father, then tugged at Cooper's arm. "Please."

He released the grip he had on the man's shirt. His hand in the small of Grace's back, he marched them toward the door.

"Grace, I suggest you watch yourself." Arthur's words hung in the air.

Cooper spun to face her father. "Are you threatening her?"

"Not at all. I'm advising my daughter to be careful."

That arrogant, egotistical, self-centered... Cooper took a deep breath in an attempt to curb his fury. He wanted to wipe the smug look off Arthur's face. The man thought he was untouchable.

Izzie flicked her hand, motioning for Cooper to keep walking. "Mr. Harrison, I believe it's in everyone's best interest if you leave. You wouldn't want to cause a scene, would you?"

Arthur straightened his shirt. "Not at all."

Cooper laced his fingers with Grace's and strode inside, leaving his sister to deal with the worthless piece of garbage otherwise known as Grace's father. His chest heaved as he struggled to gain control of his anger.

Grace tugged his hand. "Come on, let's go back to the conference room."

He followed her down the hall and into the space where they'd spent most of the afternoon. After she sat, he lowered himself onto the chair next to her.

Daniel moved from the window to his seat and stared at him, assessing.

Not now, bro. If Cooper opened his mouth, bad things might come out.

The heater kicked on and hummed in the background. Muted voices filtered in from the main office area. But the room stayed silent. Cooper laced his fingers with Grace's—the one thing keeping him grounded at the moment.

Izzie entered and closed the door behind her. "Well, that was fun—not."

"I want a restraining order against him for Grace. That man isn't coming anywhere near her again," he said through gritted teeth.

"Coop." Daniel held out a hand, palm out.

He glared at his brother. "Don't Coop me."

"All right, boys, settle down." Izzie closed the blinds and returned to her original seat. "With what I know now, I agree with the restraining order. Before you go, I'll have Grace fill out the paperwork, and I'll get it to the judge as soon as you sign it."

He nodded, still not trusting himself to be civil. He'd known about the abuse since the night in the barn, but for some reason, seeing Arthur watching the sheriff's office after Grace had almost died triggered the protective streak inside him.

Quiet lingered. Everyone appeared lost in thought.

Daniel puffed out a breath. "So, I have to ask. Could we have two crimes on our hands?"

"What do you mean?" Grace stiffened beside him.

"A killer targeting bull riders and another person out to silence you, Grace."

Her eyes widened. "You mean my father?"

Daniel shrugged. "I'm not saying it's him. I'm just thinking out loud."

"I hate to admit it, but he has a point." Cooper squeezed the back of his neck with his free hand. "Bateman died. Bull rider number five out of the way. Then, around the same time, Grace is in danger." He shifted to face her. "Either you stumbled onto something without realizing it and put yourself in the killer's crosshairs, or you came home and placed a different target on your back."

"I honestly don't know which." Grace deflated like a balloon. Her gaze darted around the table from person to person. "Where do we go from here?"

Izzie placed her hands on the table and stood. "We continue investigating the deaths, but we keep a close eye on your father. I don't like what I've heard about your childhood, and it worries me that your mother is still in that house."

"My mom? She never stepped in when he belittled me." Grace shook her head. Belittled. A kind word for the torture she'd endured. Grace seemed to consider Izzie's concern. "She didn't see him physically abuse me. He always did that in private. I never considered…my mom…is she his punching bag now?"

As much as Cooper despised Grace's mother for not protecting her, his mind churned with Izzie's statement. Could Grace's mother have suffered like she had?

"I have no idea, but I'll put out a few feelers."

"Izzie, be careful." Cooper's stomach clenched at the thought of Arthur Harrison seeking revenge.

"I have no intention of putting Grace or her mother in further danger."

"That's not what I meant, Izzie." The more he learned about Arthur Harrison, his concerns increased.

"I hear you. But this is my job." His sister gave him a knowing look. She understood the risks.

Grace pinched the bridge of her nose. Her head must be hurting as much as her heart.

"Get the restraining order paperwork. I want Gracie home so she can rest. And get me the name of the insurance agent. We'll make that visit first thing tomorrow if he or she is close to Rollins."

"I can go with you now. We don't have to wait," Grace said.

"No. I shouldn't have let you come here today. You need to let your body heal." They had a killer to find, but at the moment, Cooper cared more about the woman beside him than his job.

"Go. Rest. Come at the case fresh in the morning." Izzie sauntered to the door and tapped the frame twice. "We will find the killer and solve the mystery behind who is after Grace. I promise." His sister disappeared down the hall.

"I'll go dive into the lot of characters in this horror flick. Let me know if you need anything." Daniel followed Izzie's lead out of the room.

"I guess we should head out too." Grace stood.

The weight of the case and the confrontation with her father sat on Cooper's shoulders like a two-ton bull. He had to up his game to keep her safe. The checklist rolled through his mind. Paperwork. Get her safely to his truck. Check to see if someone had tampered with the truck. Get her home to rest.

"Let's do this." Cooper escorted Grace to Izzie's office.

God, please help me keep her safe from whoever has her in his sights.

TEN

The aroma from the flickering spiced cinnamon candle on the kitchen window ledge permeated through the room. Grace traced her finger around the coffee mug rim, allowing the familiar Christmas scent to infuse her senses. She stared at the dark liquid. Yesterday's events reeled in her mind. Cooper brought her home last night and fed her. Lexi had sat in front of the fireplace, entertaining her with stories about the ranch until Cooper had insisted Grace go to bed. The time with her daughter had her yearning for more. But did she deserve to be in her daughter's life after abandoning her? Sure, she'd had her reasons, but now they seemed selfish. Her father's action had played a large role, and she'd panicked, plain and simple. Grace inhaled. She wanted time with Lexi to discover everything about her and for the young girl to get to know her. Maybe they could form a friendship. Could Grace only be friends with Lexi? She had no idea. But her heart demanded she try.

And then there was Cooper. His attention had struck a want—a desperation—she hadn't realized she craved. Her parents had never cared for her in such a loving manner. But his compassion and kindness had filled a dry well within her. Was that what it felt like to be cherished?

Miss Hannah had introduced her to God in her early teens. He'd been her comfort during those brutal years. Then, when life had taken a crazy turn, she'd turned away from Him. No. That wasn't right. She'd gone quiet—not turning to God for help and guidance—and she slowly stopped talking to Him. Maybe it was time to stop running and face God and life head-on. She blinked. She'd spoken to God more in the past couple of days than she had since her pregnancy, and He hadn't let her down yet.

She closed her eyes. *God, I'm going to do better.* A sudden warmth of acceptance filled her chest. Yes, it was time to turn back to God. The only fatherly love she'd ever experienced. Why had she ever gone silent?

"Feeling better this morning?"

Grace lifted her head and smiled at Hannah. "Good morning. The full night's sleep worked wonders. The aches have dulled, and my mind isn't fuzzy anymore. I almost feel normal." She chuckled. "Whatever normal is."

Hannah filled a mug with the bold brew, ambled to Grace and kissed the top of her head. "I'm glad to hear that. I haven't seen Cooper that anxious since Lexi fell out of the climbing tree and sprained her ankle a couple of years back."

"I'm sure that sent him over the edge with worry." Grace had a feeling he'd panicked, and Hannah had had to tend to both her son and granddaughter.

"Of all my children, that boy has the biggest heart. Izzie has something to prove. Daniel. Well, that one…he's hiding behind the humor. I wish I knew why. And Payton, she's my quiet one these days and sticks close to the animals, which baffles me. Not the animals. She's always had a knack with them. Being the youngest, she was the most outspoken. But Cooper is the protector and caretaker of the bunch. He loves hard and feels deeply." Hannah brought her cup to her lips and took a sip. "I never understood why you two went your separate ways."

Grace choked on her drink.

"Sorry." The older woman patted her on the back.

She waved off the apology. "I guess I didn't see us as a couple back then. I mean, we had a special relationship, and you know I adored your son." Loved him was more like it. And then she'd gotten pregnant, and she'd run. By the time she'd decided to face him, it had been too late. And then there was the issue with her parents.

"Oh, honey, I'm so sorry about what your father did to you. But don't let that man ruin your second chance with Cooper."

"I'll admit we've become close over the past few days, but I'm not sure we'll ever bridge that gap. He lost his wife. I can't compete with that kind of love." She wanted to be loved but wouldn't force herself into a relationship where she would come in second.

"Grace, I'll let you in on a little secret." Hannah patted her hand. "I have no doubt Cooper loved Kaitlyn. My boy wouldn't have married her otherwise. Not with what happened between his father and me. But I can say, without hesitation, Cooper has had only one soulmate. And that's you."

"Me?" She shook her head. Hannah couldn't be right.

"That boy has loved you since he met you. I don't know what happened between you, and I won't pry. But hear this. Cooper is a man of integrity. He doesn't take love lightly, and if he loses you again, his heart will shatter."

"Hannah. I don't know what to say." Did Cooper love her, as Hannah claimed? Last night, he'd shown her what it felt like to be treasured by how he'd cared for her. His actions and attention had made her heart swell. Could they make a lasting relationship work? Especially with all the secrets surrounding Lexi.

"All I ask is that you won't walk away without searching your heart for the truth."

Unable to speak, she nodded. It seemed like all she'd done since she reunited with Cooper was dig deep into her feelings.

"Hey, you two." Cooper sauntered in, kissed his mom on the cheek and slipped onto the chair next to Grace. He smiled and clutched her hand. "Feel up to meeting with the insurance agent?"

His touch soothed the confusion swirling in her mind. The simple gesture—more than she could put into words. "Of course. I assume Izzie found a name?"

"She called an hour ago. Believe it or not, the guy's in Rollins." He glanced at his watch. "We need to be in town in about forty-five minutes."

"I can manage that." She finished her coffee in one gulp and pushed from the table. "Give me twenty minutes." She placed her mug in the sink and hurried to her temporary bedroom.

After brushing her teeth and hair and applying a little makeup to cover her bruises, she grabbed her purse and joined Cooper in the kitchen. "I'm ready."

"Then let's get moving." He entwined their fingers and led her to his truck.

She looked at their hands and smiled. This is what she'd wanted since she could remember. Someone to walk through the hard stuff in life with her. To be there when she needed support. And that person had always had a name—Cooper. She'd just been too young and naive to acknowledge it.

Fifteen minutes later, they strolled the downtown sidewalks of Rollins, Texas. Christmas wreaths adorned the streetlamps, and thick garlands hung looped from one side of the street to the other, attached at the center point where the stoplights dangled at each intersection. The Rockefeller-esque tree on the town square stood tall and proud, surrounded by oversize gifts made for children to climb on. But the pièce de résistance: the handmade nativity scene. The details—stunning. She missed the small-town feel and the effort to make the holidays special.

"The receptionist said we could find Mr. Kellin getting his morning coffee and pastry at Saddle Sips on the other side of the square."

Grace shook off the melancholy hovering over her. "I'm fine with heading over there. I haven't seen Rollins proper in a long while. I've avoided downtown."

"It's changed. Old shops closed. New shops opened. But in general, it's the same place." Cooper scanned the area. "I'm not fond of you walking through town exposed."

"Do you think my attacker would try something here?" Grace swept a hand in an arc at the businesses. The town bustled with activity even during the early hour. "Out in the open?"

"Until you were thrown in the steer pen, I

would have said no. But the killer isn't trying to be sneaky. He doesn't seem to care if it looks like an accident anymore."

Cooper's concerns dug in and took hold. She studied the people on the street. Could the killer be among them? Grace squinted. "Is that Macey over there?" She pointed to the far building on the right.

"Where?" Cooper jerked his gaze in the direction she indicated. "I don't see her."

"If it was her, she's gone now. Maybe I'm just imagining things." Now, Cooper had her paranoid.

"There's Mr. Kellin. Let's go intercept him." Cooper held her hand as they crossed the street and jogged to catch up with the man they came into town to meet. "Mr. Kellin, may we have a word?"

The man huffed. "If you need insurance, please make an appointment."

Cooper eased in front of him. "Not exactly. We're interested in a policy you wrote."

"I'm sorry. I can't discuss other clients." Kellin nudged past them and aimed for the corner crosswalk.

"Even for a police investigation?" Cooper's voice rose, catching the attention of several passersby.

That stopped the man in his tracks. He pivoted to face them. "I have no idea why the police would be interested in one of my policies."

When Cooper didn't move, Mr. Kellin's shoulders sagged. "Fine. Follow me to my office. I don't exactly want people overhearing our conversation."

"Thank you. We won't take up too much of your time." Grace glanced at Cooper.

He jutted his chin for her to follow Mr. Kellin. The trio stepped into the crosswalk.

An engine revved, and horns honked. Grace's head whipped toward the squeal of tires.

"Gracie!" Cooper wrapped his arm around her waist and threw her out of the way of the oncoming truck. He twisted and took the brunt of the fall.

A sickening thud came from the street, followed by people screaming and tires spinning on the pavement. She rolled her head and spotted Mr. Kellin. His crumpled and broken body lay mere feet away.

She struggled to slow her pulse but failed.

If not for Cooper, she would've joined Mr. Kellin in death.

Cooper's shoulder burned from the impact of the asphalt. Same blasted one from his bull-riding incident. The fall had torn his shirt and ripped the skin beneath. His arms shook as he held Grace. But white lights streaked his vision at the sight of Mr. Kellin's lifeless body. *God, thank You for not letting that be Grace.* Cooper's conscience poked at him for his relief that it was Kellin and not his Gracie, but he refused to deny the truth.

He shifted on the ground, giving Gracie space. "Are you okay?"

"I think so." Her teeth chattered. "I can't believe that happened."

"Can you move?"

Without responding, she pushed to a seated position.

"Go ahead and sit on the sidewalk curb. I'll join you in a minute." More like a hot minute. Once he got his body to cooperate. And he thought bull riding was dangerous. Going mano a mano with a truck rivaled the most brutal falls he'd ever taken in the rodeo arena. At least there, he landed on dirt. Thankfully, he hadn't hit his head.

"Cooper, are you okay?" Grace's hand rested on his arm.

"I will be." He jutted his chin toward the sidewalk. "Go. Get out of the street. I'll be there as soon as I check on Mr. Kellin." The man had met his demise, but Cooper would be negligent in his duties as an officer of the law and a human being if he didn't ensure the man was beyond help.

Grace hesitated, then complied.

Now, to figure out how to move. If he shifted one way, he'd put pressure on his shredded shoulder. If he rolled the other, he'd have to use his sore arm to push up. Deducing neither option would be less painful than the other, he struggled to sit up. A groan escaped.

"Cooper?"

"I'm good. Give me a second." He breathed in through his nose and out through his mouth to curtail the nausea threatening to make itself known.

With caution, he stood and stumbled over. The angle of Kellin's body left no doubt. And the blood? Too much. Cooper placed his fingers on Mr. Kellin's carotid pulse point. The lack of beat confirmed what Cooper had already known. The man's time on earth had ended. "Rest in peace, Kellin," Cooper whispered, then hobbled to Grace's side and lowered himself next to her. He put his good arm around her and kissed her temple. "I'm sorry."

Her eyes popped wide. "For what? Saving my life?"

"I don't know. For putting you in danger? For it happening to begin with?" He only knew that if the truck had hit her, he'd blame himself for not protecting her.

The voices and commotion around him penetrated the fog inhabiting his brain. He logged fire truck sirens in the distance and a sheriff's department SUV parked sideways, blocking the street, protecting the scene and emergency personnel. He examined the area. Had the hit-and-run driver circled back to confirm he'd completed the job? But who was the target? Kellin or Grace? He zeroed in on the far building. A man resembling Arthur Harrison tucked around the corner. Or had Cooper's imagination gotten the best of him? He clocked Izzie striding toward him and breathed a sigh of relief.

"Coop!"

He waved at his sister and winced at the pull in his arm. "We're good!" Kinda.

She jogged the final distance and halted in front of them. "You have blood on your hands and shoulder?"

"The stuff on my shoulder is mine, but on my hands—that's Mr. Kellin's. He didn't make it."

"I can see that. Someone called it in. The coroner's on the way."

"I don't know how Kellin's tied to all this, but no one should die like that."

"Agree." Feet apart and hands resting on her utility belt, she ran an assessing eye over them. "Medical?"

"I wouldn't complain." He'd reached his limit between the bull-riding incident and the hit-and-run. His body protested any and all movement at the moment.

Both Grace and Izzie jerked their gazes at him.

Izzie raised an eyebrow. "Care to share with the class?"

"Yeah, I know. I never ask for medical. But I'm not stupid. The scrapes on my shoulder need cleaning. I can't do anything for Mr. Kellin, but I can for Gracie. I want her checked out."

"I only have a few new bruises. You shielded me from the worst of it. Unlike poor Mr. Kellin over there." Grace motioned toward the dead insurance agent and stared in silence.

He understood her pondering the situation. He'd run the scenario over and over in his mind. Had he missed something that would have saved the man's life?

Izzie crouched beside Cooper and lowered her voice. "Did someone not want you to talk with him?"

Cooper shook his head, uncertain of anything anymore. His gaze never left Mr. Kellin's crumpled body. "Honestly, I'm not sure. The three of us were walking together. The driver could have targeted Grace, and Mr. Kellin was collateral damage."

Grace gasped. "He died because of me?"

"Do not take on that guilt. We do not know who the driver had his sights on." Izzie's no-nonsense tone snapped Grace's head up. "The only person responsible is the one driving the vehicle that took aim at you."

Grace nodded.

"Did you catch a license plate number, Coop?"

"It was covered in mud." He'd seen the tail of the truck as it sped away, but whoever planned the attack had thought ahead.

"Grace?"

"Sorry, no."

"We'll figure it out." When the paramedics arrived, one pair focused on Mr. Kellin's body and the other two headed their way. Izzie stood. "Once your injuries are tended to, I'll need your statements."

He rolled his eyes at his sister, the queen of understatement. "Meet you at the ranch house? Or your office?"

"The ranch." Izzie inspected the immediate area. "I don't want listening ears. I trust my department, but with how this case is going…"

Cooper agreed with his sister. Plus, Grace would be tucked out of sight. "See you there in a couple of hours?"

"That works. I have to go wrangle my deputies. I'll see you soon." Izzie turned to leave and stopped. "Don't give Tanner and Gary a hard time." With the warning in play, she strode away.

"Yo, Coop. Bulls weren't enough for you?" One of the paramedics, Tanner, dropped his duffel beside him.

"Har har." Cooper shook his head. He appreciated the levity after their harrowing experience. But couldn't quite muster more than simple responses. "Take a look at Grace first."

"Gary will be here in a sec. We can do both. Now, hush and let me do my job."

Cooper glared at the man. "Noah and Harper have better bedside manners than you."

"Yeah, yeah. I've heard it before. But y'all love me anyway."

Cooper harrumphed. "Whatever."

Gary waltzed over and gently patted him on the back, opposite the new abrasions. "Ignore my partner. He's a mess."

Grace giggled at the men's antics. Probably a stress release, but he'd take it and thank the men later for their attempt at easing the tension. The happy sound wormed its way into Cooper and warmed him from the inside out.

Cooper gritted his teeth as Tanner pulled the material from the cuts. The antiseptic brought tears to his eyes, but he blinked them back. He wouldn't complain. The man was only doing his job.

Tanner attached the final bandage to Cooper's back and taped his shirt together. The gesture allowed enough time for him to make it home and change clothes. "There ya go. Don't mess up my handiwork."

"Thanks, man." As the paramedics gathered their supplies and walked away, Cooper released a long breath and faced Grace. "Ready to head to the ranch?"

"More than." She stood and held out her hand.

He accepted her assistance and staggered to his feet.

"Whoa there, cowboy."

He brushed off her concern and laced his fingers with hers. He glanced at Mr. Kellin. The medics had placed a sheet over the man to keep the crowd from gawking. "I keep going over what happened. There was no warning."

Grace scraped her teeth along her bottom lip. The furrow in her brow deepened.

"What has you thinking so hard?"

"You know how I thought I saw Macey five minutes or so before the truck barreled down on us."

He hadn't seen Drake's girlfriend and had to take Grace's word for it. "I remember."

"What if she's involved?"

"It's feasible, I suppose. It wouldn't take long for her to circle around to her vehicle. But why target Kellin? Assuming he was the one she was after." As he mulled over the possibility, he inspected the parking lot before he led her to his truck. "We'll throw it by Izzie when she joins us at the ranch."

Grace nodded but remained quiet. Her gaze unfocused, lost in thought.

He placed his hand under her elbow and assisted her onto the passenger seat. He couldn't do anything for Mr. Kellin, but Grace's safety—he could do something about that. "I promise I'll do my best to protect you. I realize our relationship is tentative, and we have things to work out, but I don't want to lose you again."

She cupped his cheek. A sad smile brushed her lips. "Nor I you."

The warmth of her hand had him leaning into her touch. Even with all the mistreatment Grace had endured throughout her youth, she had flourished despite her father. Reality snapped him from their admission. "I want you tucked in safely back at the ranch."

She nodded and buckled her seat belt.

Cooper clicked the door shut and rounded the front of his vehicle, his eyes on a constant scan of the area, searching for the ongoing threat to Grace. One he was determined to stop before he lost her for good.

ELEVEN

Grace had cleaned up since the close call with the truck and had enjoyed a light meal Hannah forced her to consume. She admitted she felt better after the shower and food, but here in the barn with the animals—that was her comfort place. The whinny of the horses drew a smile to her face. The fat cat weaving between her legs added to relieving the stress from the horrors she'd witnessed. She could breathe deeply for the first time since they'd arrived back on the ranch.

"Can I join you?"

She spotted Lexi toeing the dirt and waved her in. "Of course."

Lexi skipped to her side. "Daddy said you had a rough afternoon." The young girl rhythmically petted Cooper's horse Rascal.

"I did but having you here with me helps." Grace hadn't lied. She longed to spend time with her daughter but hadn't pushed. The snatches of time they'd had only spurred her on to want more.

"When I miss my mom, I come to the barn."

"It's a nice place to sort out your thoughts."

Lexi smiled at her, then sobered. "I don't remember much about her."

"Your mother?"

"Yeah. More feelings than memories."

"From what I heard, you were young. It's no wonder you don't remember much."

Lexi shrugged.

Grace waited, but the young girl didn't say anything else. "Since we've just met, I'd love to know more about you."

The girl's hand stopped mid pet. "You do? Like what?"

"Oh, you know, the basics. Like what's your favorite food? Color? If you have a boyfriend." Grace held her breath that Lexi would open up and let her in.

Lexi giggled. "Boys are gross."

"Okay, then. Got it. No boyfriend."

"I like blue, pink, green, orange—"

Grace grinned. "So basically, all colors."

The girl shrugged. "I can't choose."

"I can relate. My favorites are purple, hot pink and lime green." Grace mimicked Lexi's shrug. "It's hard to pick one."

"My favorite food is pizza." Lexi scratched Rascal's nose. "What about you?"

"Pizza is good. But I think I prefer tacos."

"Oh, yes. I love tacos too. Grandma Hannah makes a taco bar every Tuesday night."

"That sounds amazing." The ease of the conversation pleased Grace. Her heart filled with love for her daughter. Maybe once the truth came out, Lexi wouldn't hate her. She could only hope and pray.

Cooper followed the sound of voices and found Grace and Lexi chattering away in the barn. He stuttered to a stop at the sight in front of him. The pair were laughing and talking nonstop while brushing the horses. A bond appeared to have formed between his daughter and her biological mother. Who would have guessed they'd have connected so quickly. Witnessing the ease had his mind jumbled. He loved Lexi and wanted to protect her from further pain. Yet, Grace had a special place in his heart, and if they continued…how would Lexi respond once he told her the truth?

"Hey, Daddy."

"Howdy, princess." He strode to his daughter's side.

"Did you know that Miss Grace loves tacos? And that she hates brussel sprouts just like me."

"In fact, I do." He glanced at Grace. A sad smile formed on her lips. "She also likes onion rings dipped in barbeque sauce." He fake shuddered.

Grace chuckled. "It's good."

"Whatever you say." He looked at Lexi and stuck out his tongue and crossed his eyes.

His daughter doubled over laughing.

He melted at the scene in front of him. Never in his wildest imagination did he dream his daughter and his first love would get along so well after such a short time. Lexi deserved to know the truth, but he refused to end the beautiful moment.

The trio spent the next half hour tending to the animals, while Grace and Lexi talked like long-lost friends.

"I think it's time for Grace and me to go in and clean up. Aunt Izzie is coming over to meet with us, and I don't think she'd be too happy if we smell like horse."

Lexi pouted. "Fine. You go do adult conversation things, and I'll finish feeding the barn cats and stuff."

"Sounds like a plan. But stay out of the stalls."

His daughter rolled her eyes. "I'm not dumb."

He leaned down and kissed her cheek. "I know that. I was just reminding you."

Lexi smiled and raced across the barn to the tack room where they kept the cat food.

"You've done a fantastic job with her." Grace's praise clogged his throat with emotion.

"Thanks. But Kaitlyn is the one responsible."

"I'm sure she did her fair share, but I only have to watch the two of you to know you're a great dad."

Unsure his voice would hold up, he nodded. Now to make the biggest dad decision of his life.

Tell Lexi soon or wait and see Grace's plans for the future. He would not allow his daughter to be hurt by anyone, including her mother.

After washing up from tending to the horses, Grace relaxed against Cooper on the couch in the ranch house living room while waiting on Izzie to arrive. His fingers brushed up and down her arm in a soothing stroke. Years ago, she'd dreamed of being in his arms, and here she was. But for how long? She hoped forever, but nothing had ever gone her way in her personal life. She closed her eyes, soaking in his warmth. The time with horses had given her a reprieve from the hit-and-run earlier. Neither she nor Cooper had said a word in the last twenty minutes or so. Her mind spun, focusing on the accident. The mystery of who the driver had targeted bothered her. Her? Or Mr. Kellin? Had they tripped over the answer to the crime when they discovered the insurance policy?

"You're doing it again."

She lifted her gaze to Cooper. "What?"

"Thinking too hard." He squeezed her hand.

"Just trying to fit the puzzle pieces together."

Cooper hummed in agreement.

"You two look better." Izzie ambled in and dropped onto the recliner.

"And you look tired." Cooper leaned forward and put his elbows on his knees.

Grace immediately missed the connection. "Did you find the driver?"

"That's why I'm here." Izzie scrubbed her face, then dragged her hands to her chin. "We found the truck and the driver."

Cooper jolted. "Who? Where?"

"About three miles from downtown. The driver wrapped the truck engine around a tree. The accident shouldn't have been fatal. The vehicle hadn't hit that hard. But since the driver hadn't worn a seat belt..." Izzie shrugged. "She was thrown from the truck and broke her neck."

Grace gasped. "She?"

Izzie nodded. "The impact threw Macey Webster six feet from the truck. The medical examiner said she died instantly."

Cooper scowled. "Who was her target?"

"Believe it or not, we think both Grace and Mr. Kellin. We found several text messages with Kellin about the insurance policy and what appear to be surveillance photos of Grace."

"Two birds, one stone type of thing?" Cooper asked.

"That would be my guess. My deputies are working both scenes. I came to get your statements and let you know about Macey." Izzie pulled her phone from her pocket. "I'm going to record your account of what happened if that's okay. I'm too exhausted to take notes."

"I don't have a problem with that." Grace understood the fatigue.

She and Cooper tag-teamed the series of events.

"That's it. That's all I can remember." Cooper shifted on the couch.

Grace studied him. The man's gashes on his shoulder had to sting.

"One more thing." Izzie slouched in her seat. "I personally served the restraining order to your father. He wasn't happy, to say the least."

"I can imagine his response." And glad she hadn't been within his reach once he read the document. She cringed at the anticipated resulting blow from the delivery of the news.

"It did not go over well." Izzie closed her eyes and breathed deep. "Your mother witnessed the whole thing."

"Did she try to defend him?"

"Not at all."

Now, that shocked Grace. But then again, they'd toyed with the idea her mother had experienced her father's wrath as well. "What'd she say?"

"Contradicting Arthur's refusal for us to enter, Ava requested we come in. Once my deputy and I sat in the living room, she asked us to wait and excused herself. The action confused me at the time, but I went with it. Arthur and I had a lengthy stare-down. About twenty minutes later, your mother returned with two large suitcases."

Grace stiffened. Cooper placed his hand on her knee, and she relaxed a smidge.

"Ava requested a ride to the sheriff's office to file a restraining order of her own." Izzie tapped her phone on her palm. "Your mother stated that Arthur berated her for years, but when you left for college, he began to physically abuse her."

Grace's stomach threatened to revolt. She didn't have warm feelings toward her mother but wouldn't wish her father's hatred on her worst enemy. "My leaving caused him to hit mom?"

"No. Absolutely not." Cooper gripped her cold hand. "This is not on you."

Her head knew that, but her heart screamed with guilt. "The result is the same whether it's my fault or not."

"Grace." Izzie's soft tone pulled Grace from the ensuing outburst. "Your father has a problem. Neither you nor your mother are responsible for his actions."

She chewed on the inside of her cheek, processing the entire conversation. "What happens now?"

"My department will investigate the claims. Apparently, your mother visited the doctor multiple times secretly against your father's wishes. Plus, she kept a journal that will help us prove your father's domestic violence guilt."

"She's pressing charges?" Cooper asked.

"Yes. She made it abundantly clear that if I can

deliver enough evidence to make the conviction stick, she'd testify against him."

"Good. Arthur deserves to go to jail." Cooper's voice held a scary edge to it. One she'd never heard before.

"That he does. Now, if you'll excuse me, the job is calling." Izzie left Grace and Cooper to mull over the latest news.

Grace sagged into the couch cushions. *Go, Mom.* But could she do the same? She had no idea. The fact was she wouldn't have to. Even though the statute of limitations on physical abuse hadn't run out, nor had it on attempted murder, she had no proof. No one had witnessed or seen the evidence of his attacks. Her own naivete and her father's threats prevented her from filing charges.

One problem down, or at least pushed to the back of her worries, thanks to her mother standing up to her father and Izzie's insistence that Grace file a restraining order. Now, to see if her father played a prominent role in the attacks on her or if someone else wanted her dead.

Cooper stared at the fireplace and the colorful stockings hanging from the mantel. Two weeks until Christmas Day. Lexi loved the holidays, and he had fallen short this year due to the circumstances. His mom had stepped up and made cookies with her granddaughter and decorated the house until it looked like Christmas threw up in every room. But his heart hated the fact that he hadn't done the special things himself. But with Grace's life at risk, he'd let go of that guilt.

Lexi had grown close to Grace in the short time Grace had stayed at the ranch house. The scene he'd walked into at the barn was proof of that. Maybe the truth wouldn't hold such a punch once his daughter knew his secret. What if he gave her the extra special gift of revealing that Grace was her biological mom? Was he ready for that? Yes. Perhaps. Who knew?

Cooper had no doubt in his mind that he was ready to keep Grace close for a lifetime. The woman had stolen his heart years ago. He never wanted to lose her again. As for marriage? Not yet. But the possibility had crossed his mind multiple times. He'd broach the subject of telling Lexi in a little bit. For now, he'd let the news Izzie provided settle.

"How are you taking your mother's actions?" he asked.

"I'm surprised. It's making me rethink how I feel about her. I'm happy she has the courage to do it. I don't think I could have."

"You were young then. Age and experience give wisdom. You're stronger and braver now."

"Maybe so, but I'm dreading the gossip." Grace leaned her head back on the couch. "I can't wait to leave. Get away from the memories of my home life. Plus, the looks of pity that will come once the truth about my father comes to light."

Cooper jerked his gaze toward her. She was leaving him and Lexi? Anger pooled in his belly. And to think he had envisioned a future with her and had almost agreed to tell Lexi the truth. He glanced around, ensuring no one listened. "I understand not wanting to live through the questions, but I'm glad we didn't reveal our secret."

"What?" Grace shifted. Her mouth open.

"Disappearing from my life is one thing but telling Lexi, then leaving? No. You are not hurting my daughter like that." Her announcement had punched the air from his lungs. Her current stunned expression barely registered. His life had shattered into pieces. He had to get out of there before his mouth got the best of him. "If you'll excuse me."

"Cooper?"

"Not now." He marched out of the living room and aimed for the kitchen while he still held a thin grip on his fury. He yanked out a chair and plopped down. Head in his hands, he rested his elbows on the table, regretting his earlier thoughts. Why had he allowed his heart to get involved? No. This wasn't about him. It was about his daughter. Lexi deserved a mom who'd stay by her side when things got tough.

"Cooper James Sinclair. What did you say

to Grace?" His mother's scolding tone ripped through him.

He gritted his teeth. "Nothing that wasn't true."

"Somehow, I don't believe that. That girl rushed out the door and raced to the barn like a pack of wolves chased her."

He shrugged. Mustering an ounce of sympathy was beyond his ability. Grace planned to walk away from Lexi. From him. "What can I say? The truth hurts." Boy, he knew that firsthand.

"That woman loves you." His mom slipped into a chair next to him.

"Sometimes that's not enough."

She tilted her head. "If you're worried she doesn't love her daughter, then you're a fool."

He whipped his head up and stared wide-eyed at his mother. "She told you?"

"Grace? No." Hannah shook her head. "As if you could hide the fact Lexi is Grace's child." She tsked.

His heart pounded like a stampede of cattle. "How long have you known?"

Mom covered his hand with hers. "Honey, the moment I saw that precious baby, I knew. But you and Kaitlyn refused to correct the assumptions your brother and sisters made, so I went with it. I figured you had a good reason for keeping your secret." His mother had stayed silent for eight years. She'd never, not once, exposed his and Kaitlyn's untold truth.

The story poured from his lips. He didn't leave anything out. From Grace walking away without telling him, to Kaitlyn's selfless sacrifice. "In the end, that's why we stuck with the theory. We did it for Grace." He stared at the red candle and holly centerpiece. "Are you mad?"

"Oh, my darling boy, Kaitlyn was an excellent mother and wife. She loved you with a passion most mothers can only hope for their sons. And as a mother—Lexi has always been loved. Unlike Grace. That girl's life…" Hannah sighed. "We all failed her."

As much as his mother's words penetrated his heart, he refused to let go of the internal wounds. "That doesn't give her the right to come in and out of Lexi's life on a whim."

His mom tilted her head and studied him like an ant under a microscope. "Now that the truth is out, let's not stop with Lexi's parentage."

"What are you suggesting?" Confused, he stared at his mother, attempting to interpret her words.

"I'm sure you're concerned about your daughter. Like any good father would be. But let's not cloud the real reason you're upset."

He blinked at her, trying his hardest to digest her words. "Meaning?"

"You've loved Grace since you both were teens. Your fear centers around her leaving you—again."

He shook his head. "I—"

Hannah held up her palm. "Stop. I can handle a lot of things, but don't lie to me or yourself anymore."

Denial sat on his lips. But the truth looped in his head. "She ghosted me, mom. I gave her my heart. My everything."

Contrary to popular belief around town, Grace had been his one and only. He'd thought after that night, she'd be his forever. "And she disappeared. I looked for her in the carved-out spare moments during the academy, but she'd hidden herself too well. Then I found out I almost lost out on Lexi's life. It shredded me. I can't do that again."

His mother tilted her head and looked him straight in the eye. "Then Kaitlyn scooped up all those pieces and glued them back together."

He'd fallen apart when he couldn't locate Grace, but he'd been shattered when he'd discovered her betrayal. Kaitlyn had become his constant. Always beside him. Always holding him up. "She did. I *did* love her."

"I know you did. And Kaitlyn loved you and Lexi. I was proud to call her family. We all mourned the day she died. But let's be honest. Grace has been and always will be your soulmate." His mom squeezed his fingers. "I don't think Grace has any intention of leaving you or Lexi."

"But she said she couldn't wait to leave and get away from the memories." Okay, so he sounded like a whiny little boy. So what? Grace had stomped on his heart.

"Son, that girl meant get away from her father and go back to the city where she lives. Not far from where you and Lexi live, by the way. Not to escape you or Lexi. This town let her down. No one saw what was right in front of them. She may have fond memories of the ranch, but Rollins... That will take time to heal. Now that her mother spoke up and left that no-good man, maybe Grace can put it behind her for good."

Cooper searched deep in his heart and realized his mother spoke the truth. His fears and hurt had dictated his spiteful words. He owed Grace an apology.

"I have to find her. Talk to her. Pray that it's not too late." He pushed from the table.

"You know I will." Hannah smiled. "Go. Get your girl."

God, please don't let my stupidity push her away for good. I love her.

TWELVE

Cooper's words had hit their target. The man Grace loved had ripped holes in her heart. Once she found her ability to fill her lungs with air, she grabbed her coat and rushed to the barn, to the horses that never let her down. To the unconditional love of the animals she craved her entire life.

God, it hurts so bad.

At least she'd begun to find her way back to God, her friend and confidant. The unconditional love of a father, unlike her own.

Cooper's brush-off replayed in Grace's head. The dismissal had gutted her. What had she said or done to make him close down like that? She wiped a stray tear from her cheek with her gloved hand. A bone-deep exhaustion from erecting another wall around her heart settled in. She was so tired of protecting herself from the emotional roller coasters in her life. She adjusted her balance in the saddle, then clicked her tongue and nudged Dusty's ribs. The borrowed horse galloped across the pasture away from the barn. The crisp winter air cooled her cheeks and tamped down her anger. However, it did nothing for the ache in her heart. She gripped the reins and edged the gelding toward the river at the far end of the property. A place that held fond memories.

Maybe she should have stayed close to the ranch house until Izzie officially closed the case. But Macey was dead, and with the 9mm in the saddle pouch and the critter cams, along with the ranch hands working in the area, Grace should be safe for a brief ride. Clearing her head before she said something she couldn't take back was a necessity. She'd reached her limit with Cooper's attitude and skepticism. Hadn't she suffered enough over the years? He had no right to keep Lexi from knowing the truth.

"Ahh! Why?" Tears blurred her vision. She knew why. She'd abandoned their daughter. Not because she didn't want Lexi but to protect her from Grace's father. Grace had panicked when she discovered the pregnancy and vowed never to let Arthur Harrison touch the child.

That was nine years ago. Since then, her life had changed. She had changed. She'd become stronger—braver. She owned her own company. Was a successful businesswoman. How could Cooper not see that? But no, he threw her mistake in her face and stormed off.

She sucked in the cool air, stinging her lungs,

and reined in Dusty to a trot. Her words from earlier ripped through her memory. *I can't wait to leave. Get away from my past.*

No wonder Cooper put the brakes on telling Lexi. She hadn't meant *leave* Cooper or Lexi, just that she wanted to go home to Lackard. She hated being this close to her father. The man triggered insecurities she'd fought hard to overcome.

She slowed the horse to a halt near the edge of the woods. Grace leaned forward and hugged his neck. "Thanks, Dusty. You're exactly what I needed."

The clomp of horse hooves galloping in the distance grabbed her attention. Great. Had Cooper come to scold her for riding out here alone? She shifted in the saddle, causing it to creak. Lexi's black hair flowed behind her as the horse rushed toward Grace.

"Miss Grace, wait up!" Lexi closed the distance and reined in her horse next to Dusty.

"What are you doing out here?" Grace scanned the pasture for Cooper. "Does your father know?"

"I came to see you without him around."

Grace didn't want another thing added to Cooper's mad-at-her list, but she couldn't turn Lexi away. She narrowed her gaze at the girl. "Why don't you want your father with you?"

"Look, can we take a walk and...um...maybe talk?" Lexi nibbled on her lower lip. A habit similar to Grace's when she was worried or deep in thought.

She studied Lexi, wondering how much trouble they'd both be in with Cooper if she didn't let him know where his daughter…their daughter… was. "For a little while. Once your father realizes you took off on horseback, he'll have every ranch hand out searching for you." Grace decided she'd give Lexi five minutes, then she'd call Cooper.

"Thank you." Lexi slid off her horse and let the reins dangle to the earth. "You can let Dusty go too. He and Stormy won't wander off."

Grace joined her daughter on the ground and patted Dusty. He and Stormy nosed each other but stayed close. "All right, you have my attention. What do you want to talk about?"

Lexi toed the ground with her boot. "I lost my mom four years ago."

"That had to be hard on you at such a young age." From what Grace had heard about Kaitlyn, Lexi had lost a loving mom.

"It was. But Dad's the best. He's made sure I'm loved enough for two parents and—" Lexi chuckled "—he even learned how to do all the girly stuff."

Grace grinned. She could picture Cooper researching how to be a girl dad. "He watched videos online to learn how to braid your hair and paint your nails, didn't he?"

The girl's jaw dropped. "How did you know that?"

"Because that's the kind of guy your dad is." She'd known that firsthand as a teen.

"That's true. He works hard, then comes home and takes care of me. It's hard on him, and I know he's lonely. Has been since Mom died. I'm worried about him." The sadness in the young girl's eyes made Grace want to weep. Lexi's insight was far beyond her years.

Grace clasped her daughter's hands in hers. The fact she was touching and talking to her child, a child she'd never thought she'd see again, hit her square in the chest. She inhaled, willing the ache away. "If I could, I'd give you back your mom. From everything I've heard, she was an amazing, selfless woman."

Kaitlyn had jumped in and taken the role of mother to a newborn without a second thought, raising Lexi as her own. Never once correcting the assumptions to protect Cooper and, by extension, Grace. She owed Kaitlyn a huge debt of gratitude.

"So, this chat is about concern for your father?"

"I mean, I am worried about him, but no." Lexi shook her head, then sighed. "Mom bought a jewelry box for me when she found out she had cancer. Dad gave it to me for my birthday this year. He wanted me to have it but asked me not to wear the jewelry outside the house until I turned sixteen.

He's worried I'll lose it." Lexi swallowed hard. "Mom left me a heart locket necklace with her and dad's picture in it and a diamond bracelet for when I got older. It was her grandmother's. Dad told me about it when I asked. According to Grandma Hannah, the box is a miniature hope chest."

"That's special that you have that." If possible, Grace's opinion of Kaitlyn amplified.

Lexi nodded. "What Grandma Hannah and Dad don't know is I found a letter under the velvet bottom of the box."

Oh, that poor girl. Words from the grave couldn't be easy for her. She'd somehow drop a hint to Cooper about the note from Kaitlyn. "Did you read it?"

Lexi nodded. "The envelope said I wasn't supposed to open it until I turned eighteen. But you know me..." The girl spread her arms wide. "I'm curious."

Grace smiled. "Wonder where you got that from?"

The corner of Lexi's mouth lifted. "My mother."

Tears pricked Grace's eyes. *More than you realize, my little girl.* The desire to reveal the truth hung like a thunderstorm over her head. "What did the letter say? If you don't mind my asking."

"Mom told me that she and Dad had a secret, and she trusted me not to tell my Grandma Hannah or my aunts and uncles. But I want to tell you."

Grace's heart thumped at the gesture. "I'm honored you want to share. But are you sure you want to tell me what she said?"

Lexi stared at her boots and remained quiet for several minutes, appearing to either mull over her choice or to gain courage. Grace wasn't sure which.

"She told me that dad was my dad, but she wasn't my biological mom."

Grace's stomach flipped. "And how do you feel about that?"

"I'm confused." Lexi lifted her gaze. "Mom loved me, and I loved her. What I can remember, anyway." She shrugged. "But I guess I wonder why my biological mother didn't want me?"

Oh wow, Grace couldn't do this. Not without Cooper. She'd promised him. However, the way Lexi studied her... Did the girl already know? Had Kaitlyn let the proverbial cat out of the bag? "Did she tell you who?"

Lexi opened her mouth to speak.

"Hold on." The bushes to Grace's right rustled. She slipped her phone from her pocket and opened the critter cam app Cooper had insisted she install. A figure crept closer to where she and Lexi stood. "We have to get out of here."

Lexi's eyes widened. "Someone's out there?"

"Yes. Now, come on." Grace grabbed Lexi's hand, and the pair ran in the opposite direction of where the camera picked up the trespasser, choosing not to use the horses. The path to the barn would lead them out in the open for an extended time.

They sprinted through the woods, leaping over logs and tree limbs blocking their path. Grace knew the property, but the area where they'd stopped riding only had two directions to go. Either into the pasture with no coverage or through the trees to the river. The icy water had no appeal, especially this time of year, but running through the open land had death written all over it.

Grace yanked Lexi behind a huge tree and held a finger to her lips. Her chest heaved at the exertion. If they weren't careful, the person sneaking around would hear their breathing.

"Stay still," she whispered and lifted the phone to call Cooper for help. Making sure no one had found them before hitting speed dial, she peeked around the trunk.

A large stick swung at her head.

Grace ducked. "Run!" She jerked Lexi with her and took off. Her phone lay on the ground near the tree where she'd avoided the attacker's attempt to hit her. Cooper had no idea trouble had found her and Lexi. They were on their own.

Nowhere to go except the river and no way to call for help. How would she protect her daughter?

God, I need You. Lexi needs You. Please send Cooper to help us. I'm trusting You with my daughter.

* * *

"Grace?" Cooper swung the barn door closed behind him. The crisp, cool air mingled with the scent of hay. "Gracie, I'm sorry." He searched the interior and came to two empty stalls. Great. Lexi's horse was gone, too. The pair must be together. *Grace, please don't tell our daughter the truth. Not without me.* He should have known Grace would instinctively go for a ride. For as long as he could remember, horseback had been her go-to for comfort when the world got too heavy.

Soft nickers and snorts filled the otherwise silent barn. Dust particles floated in the air, amplified by the light streaming through the open shutters on the stalls.

Where had they gone? Maybe Grace had texted him. He hoped so, but deep down, he knew he grasped at the improbability. Not after the way he'd treated her. Cooper patted his pockets anyway, searching for his phone. He must have left it in the house. He sighed and moved to his horse Rascal. "I let my insecurities get to me, didn't I?"

Rascal's head bobbed up and down.

"I know, boy." He ran a hand over the horse's neck. "I messed up. I shouldn't have overreacted. I don't want Lexi hurt." He bowed his head. "No, that's not right. I don't want Lexi to get hurt, but Mom was right. I haven't let go of the sting from Grace abandoning both of us."

"There you are." Izzie rushed into the barn, waving his phone. "You left this on the kitchen table."

He put his hand out. "Thanks."

"Not so fast." She held the phone over her head. "I have news."

Cooper wiggled his fingers. "Give it. Then tell me what you found out."

She slapped it into his palm. "Grace's office manager, Cameron, called a few minutes ago. By the way, he's really good at his job."

"Izzie." His sister's tangents were legendary.

"Sorry. The insurance policy that Bateman thought Wrangler's Way Ventures had taken out is attached to a shell corp and not his sponsorship company. According to Cameron, the documents looked legit. There was no reason for Bateman to question the owner of the policy since it's his sponsor. Cameron's making an assumption, but he thinks Macey set Bateman up. He didn't sign the policy until after he started dating her. This is a similar situation with the other deaths as well. With the exception of Barry Larsen, whose insurance money went straight to his girlfriend, Sydney Zorn. Cameron also confirmed that Macey was involved with the plan targeting Bateman. She was one of two names that appeared on the shell corp documents."

"Two dead cowboys linked to two girlfriends?"

Cooper scratched the stubble on his jaw. "Were the women in cahoots together?"

Izzie shook her head. "It gets better. Think chameleon."

"Izzie, stop with the riddles. Just tell me." His patience had all but disappeared.

"Sydney Zorn and Macey Webster are the same person. If we dig deeper into Ryan Brown's death, I'm guessing we find a third persona for Macey. Possibly for Lance and Brent as well."

"A black widow."

"That's my take on it."

"Why go after Grace?"

"Well, it's not her father. After I served the restraining order and questioned the man, I confirmed his alibi for the attempts on her life. They held up. It's not him."

Cooper tipped his cowboy hat up and scratched his head. "So, Macey—Sydney—whatever her name is, she was the one?"

"Yes and no."

"Wait. You said one of two. Who was the other?" Man, his brain was slow today.

Izzie puffed out a mouthful of air. "She partnered with Chris Reyes. He's the second name."

"Chris? Why on earth would Chris kill other bull riders?"

"I'm still gathering information, but from what I can tell, his involvement was twofold. One, to get rid of the younger riders threatening his status. He's had several injuries, and the payouts from bull riding aren't coming in like they used to. And two, for the insurance money. Young cocky cowboys were an easy target. Especially with Macey seducing them."

Cooper rubbed his forehead. "That's just ridiculous. Bull riding is a young man's sport. Why not go out with dignity?"

"I don't know, bro. It's all kinds of wrong."

"So for both reasons, it's all about the money."

"It appears so."

Cooper let the latest theory marinate for a moment. The information made sense to a degree. He couldn't ignore the evidence. But he struggled with one detail. "The question remains. Why target Grace?"

"I'm purely guessing here. But I think Grace got too close at the last rodeo without realizing it. When Macey or Chris—who knows—saw her at Bateman's camper when he collapsed, the pair panicked."

"And tried to take Grace out, making it look like rodeo accidents until that didn't work."

Izzie pointed at him. "Exactly."

Cooper's phone beeped.

Izzie gestured to his hand. "That thing's beeped several times. Are you going to answer it?"

"That's not a text. That's the security cameras on the property." His heart rate skyrocketed. "Grace and Lexi are out riding."

Izzie rushed to his side and peered over his shoulder.

"There." He tapped on the image. "Someone's on the property. We have to get to the girls." He grabbed a bridle and hurried to Rascal.

"I'll get the ATV." Izzie sprinted from the barn.

Gunshots echoed through the air.

"Sorry, Rascal, no time for a saddle." He slipped the reins on, swung his leg over the horse and nudged the animal's ribs. "Let's go, boy." Cooper clicked his tongue, and Rascal shot through the door and into the pasture.

Cooper hadn't ridden bareback in a long time and had to focus on his balance. He leaned forward and talked to his horse. "Lexi and Grace are in trouble." Rascal appeared to understand the urgency and galloped across the dried grass without further prodding.

When Cooper reached the edge of the field where it met the woods, he dismounted. Ducking low, he sprinted toward where he'd seen the trespasser on the cameras. His knees weakened at the hum of an engine in the distance. Izzie would be there soon for backup.

"Chris, don't do this." Grace's voice cut through the trees.

He veered off in that direction.

"Shut up!"

A strangled cry made Cooper stumble. *God, please don't let anything happen to Grace. I love her. I can't lose her.* He sucked in a breath. He loved her with everything in him. How had he suppressed the truth all these years?

He slowed and peeked through the branches of the closest brush.

"Dad?" Lexi whispered to his left.

He crept to his daughter and wrapped her in a hug. "Are you all right?"

She squeezed him tight. "I'm fine. But you have to save Grace."

"That's the plan. Your Aunt Izzie is on the way. Stay here and wait for her." He released her and turned to leave.

Lexi grabbed his arm. "Be careful, Dad."

He kissed her forehead. "Count on it, princess." Easing around the trees, he stepped lightly on the leaf-covered ground toward Chris and Grace. He peered into an opening near the river. The scene in front of him stole the air from his lungs and dropped him to his knees.

The gun pressed against Grace's head had his lunch threatening to come up. The woman he loved stood there, teeth gritted. The look in her eyes—not fear but rage.

That's it, honey. Stay angry.

"I want to know who you told." Chris's fingers tightened on the gun's grip.

"Why? So you can kill someone else too? No thank you."

"I can't leave any witnesses. No one can know.

Answer me!" Spittle flew from Chris's mouth. "Who did you tell?"

Cooper crept closer while the two argued. *Come on, Gracie, keep the man talking.* He stopped behind a bush a few feet away.

"Now I get it. You and Macey were in this together, weren't you? I knew Macey looked familiar. I saw the two of you talking together at the last rodeo. But not as you and Macey but as you and Sydney. Her disguise was good, but you can't hide nature." Grace continued to taunt him.

Chris jammed the gun harder against her temple. "If you'd kept your nose out of it, we wouldn't be here right now. Stop yapping and tell me what I want to know!"

Grace ignored Chris's demands. "You're the one who brought attention to yourself."

"What are you talking about?"

"I hadn't made the connection to either of you. In fact, if you'd both stayed quiet, no one would have been the wiser. You did this to yourself." Grace's voice had risen several decibels.

"I told you to shut up!"

Cooper slid the Glock from his holster. The wild look in Chris's eyes told him he couldn't wait any longer. The man was done waiting for Grace to tell him what he wanted to know. Cooper held out the gun and stepped from his hiding spot. "Put the gun down, Chris."

The man jerked and spun himself and Grace.

"No!" He yanked her tighter against his chest and dug the barrel of the gun deeper into Grace's skin. "Leave, or I'll kill her."

Cooper kept the weapon steady and took two slow steps closer. A thought popped into his head about Macey's accident. She hadn't died in the wreck. Chris had killed her. "Like you did Macey? Did she become a liability?"

"Her name was Taylor. I loved her. She was my fiancée. But she risked everything by failing to make Grace's death look like an accident. No one was supposed to know what we had done."

"You killed the woman you loved. For what? Money? To save yourself?" Cooper's number one priority was getting Grace away from the man, but he wanted answers as well. If he kept the man talking, maybe they'd have enough proof to close the case and bring closure to the families of the cowboys who died at Chris and Macey's hands.

"Her action exposed our business."

"So, she had to die?" Cooper inched closer.

"I couldn't let her mistake ruin me."

Hadn't Cooper done that on a smaller scale? His own fear and probably a touch of pride had him spewing awful words at Grace. He had to save her. Had to apologize for his behavior. "Instead of accepting your own responsibility, you eliminated the person you loved."

"Enough!" Chris tugged her backward.

"Look, there's no escaping. We know what you did. Turn yourself in so no one gets hurt."

Chris shook his head. "Not happening." He edged closer to the small drop-off next to the river. "She's first. Then you. No one is walking away."

Grace's gaze shifted to a spot on his right.

He tossed a quick look to where her focus had shifted. Izzie. Her own weapon raised. "It's over, Chris."

A smirk lifted the corner of Chris's lips. "You're right—it *is* too late." The look in the man's eyes confirmed he planned to go down shooting.

Cooper's stomach dropped to his toes. "No, don't do it."

Grace stared at him and gave him a slight nod.

The woman had a plan. He just hoped it didn't get her killed. But he'd be ready for whatever she had in mind.

A moment later, Grace brought her arm forward, then jammed her elbow into Chris's stomach. With a quick twist, the gun no longer pointed at her head. Cooper pulled the trigger and hit the man center mass.

Chris's eyes widened. He gasped and stumbled backward. A second before going over the edge of the small cliff, he grasped Grace's shirt and yanked her into the river below.

"No! Save my mom!" Lexi ran to the drop-off.

Cooper rushed to his daughter and grabbed her before she fell. "Lexi?"

"Save her, please." Tears spill over his daughter's lashes. How had she discovered the truth?

Izzie wrapped an arm around Lexi, holding her from a dangerous fall into the water. "I've got her. Go."

He handed his sister his gun, kicked off his boots, and jumped into the cold Texas river. When he hit the water, the icy temperature stole his breath. He fought the urge to suck air into his lungs and shot to the surface. The slow-moving current was a blessing. His gaze scanned the water. Where had Grace gone? There. He spotted blond hair spread across the water. Her head back, facing the sky. The red tinted water sent his heart racing.

"Gracie!" He pulled quick strokes to her side and slipped his arms under her. "I've got you." The gash on her forehead bled, but otherwise she seemed free of other injuries.

"Cooper, don't leave me?" Her words slurred a bit.

"I'm here, honey. I'm not going anywhere. Ever." He treaded water, struggling to reposition his grip on his precious cargo—the icy water already affecting his abilities.

"Okay." Her teeth chattered. "I'm so cold."

"I know, honey. Hang on a little longer."

"'Kay." Her eyes closed. Between the hit on the head and the adrenaline dump, the temperature had sunk in its claws.

The limpness of her body had his heart pounding. Unlike her, adrenaline coursed through his veins, giving him an edge. But time was running out for both of them. The sluggishness from the effects of the cold water struck anew a sense of urgency, spurring him on. He fought the water and his muscles as he swam to the bank and lifted her into his arms. His sock feet flopped on the uneven ground. He stumbled but remained upright.

"Cooper!" Izzie yelled from somewhere above him.

"Down here!" He willed his legs to keep going. Hypothermia would burrow into both of them and not let go if they didn't get warm—fast.

"I'm bringing the ATV. Go twenty feet to your right. The land levels out there."

"Got it." He had no idea if his sister heard his response. He had to hoard every piece of his waning energy to get them to the clearing. *God, You're the only way I'm going to make it that distance. I need Your strength.*

The whining engine of the ATV had never sounded so good.

Cooper pushed his body beyond its limits. He had to save Grace. He'd lost Kaitlyn. No way would he lose the woman he'd loved as a teen. The one he'd fallen in love with all over again.

"Don't leave me, Gracie. I love you. I always have," he whispered in her ear.

"Daddy!" Lexi rushed to his side and placed a

hand under his elbow to help steady him. "Is she going to be okay?"

"If I have anything to say about it, she is." His body had hit its limit, but he pushed forward, unwilling to drop the woman who meant the world to him.

"Get in." Izzie helped him into the rear of the ATV where he collapsed onto the seat, never letting go of Grace. "I've called for medical. They'll meet us at the house."

Lexi leaned over the seat and clasped Grace's hand. "Stay with us, Miss Grace. I want to get to know my mom."

Cooper's gaze jerked to Lexi, but her focus stayed on Grace. He exhaled. Truth be told, he didn't care how Lexi found out. All he wanted was for Gracie to wake up.

He closed his eyes and drifted on the verge of sleep due to the cold seeping into his bones. Had he got to her in time? Or would Lexi lose another mother, and he lose another woman he loved?

THIRTEEN

Flames danced in the fireplace, and the logs crackled, radiating heat into the living room at the ranch house. Grace sat on the couch and stared at the Christmas stockings hanging from the mantel, wondering if she'd ever be warm again. The unexpected dip in the cold Texas river had chilled her to the bone. Grace had woken once they arrived at the ranch house. Hannah had taken one look at her and with Izzie's help had assisted her into a toasty bath. When paramedic Harper arrived, she butterflied the cut on Grace's forehead shut, then checked her over and deemed that the warm water had done its job in bringing her core temperature up. A protein bar helped counteract the faded adrenaline and boosted her energy a bit. Harper had encouraged a trip to the hospital, but Grace protested. She wanted to curl up under a blanket and pretend the near-death experience hadn't happened. In the end, Harper and Hannah stopped pushing her to seek further medical help and did what they could to ensure she'd recover from her harrowing experience.

The whole ordeal left her exhausted. She tugged the dark green fleece blanket that Cooper had wrapped her in tighter around herself, leaned back and closed her eyes. Chris holding the gun to her head and the fall into the icy water played like a movie reel in her head. Shivers racked her body at how close she'd come to dying.

"You're still cold." Cooper strode to a basket on the side of the fireplace, grabbed another blanket and tucked it around her, mummifying her in the warmth. He had showered and now wore sweatpants and a sweatshirt after their dip in the river. Unlike her, the man seemed unaffected by the frigid temperatures they'd endured. The difference in body mass probably had something to do with it. Maybe gaining a few pounds wouldn't be a bad thing. Either way, she hoped to be warm soon.

The cold penetrated deep, but the memories of what she'd lived through were the culprit of her chill. At least at the moment. "Thanks." The small acknowledgment tapped her strength. She had begun to wonder if her fatigue had more to do with a touch of depression than the icy swim.

He picked up a mug she hadn't noticed he'd brought with him when he entered the living room. "Drink this. It's Mom's special hot chocolate."

She wormed her hands out of the cocoon of the covers and accepted the cup. Lifting the chocolatey goodness to her lips, she took a sip. Hannah's special ingredient of peppermint awoke Grace's taste buds. The sugar would boost her energy, she hoped. "Just as I remember—delicious."

"Mom makes the best hot cocoa."

Grace nodded and took another sip. Heat infused her from the inside out.

"The paramedics checked you over, but I have to ask. Are you okay?" Cooper sat beside her on the couch and placed his hand on her double blanket-covered knee. His gentle touch, a balm to her heart.

"I'll be fine once I'm not freezing anymore." Assuming her brain would allow her to tone down her anxiety from Chris's actions.

"He didn't hurt you?" Cooper dropped his chin to his chest. "Retract that. I know he hurt you. But is there anything you're not telling me?" The poor man looked like someone had told him his horse died.

"Seriously, Cooper, I'm okay. Battered and bruised, but nothing I'm not used to. Although, it's been a while." She felt more than saw him stiffen next to her. Too tired to apologize for her bluntness, she let the statements hang in the air and stared at the yellow and red tendrils of fire reaching toward the flue. Fourteen years, one hundred seventy-three months or five thousand two hundred sixty-six days, but who was counting. The day she'd walked out the front door for college had likely saved her life. Arthur's consequences for disobedience had become harsher each year. She never understood why. And that bothered her.

"Ah, Gracie. I'm so sorry."

"Nothing to be sorry for. I might not like my father, but I survived. I'm stronger now. And after coming back and facing my past, I know what I want in life." She handed him her mug and shifted to face him.

He placed the cup on the coffee table and laced their fingers together. "And what's that?" His gaze met hers. Hope glimmered in his eyes. She prayed—yes, prayed—she hadn't misread his future dreams. She and God were back on speaking terms and so much more.

"I—"

"Dad!" Lexi ran into the room. She stared at their interlocked hands. A smirk twisted her lips. "Sorry. But Grandma said that Miss Grace's mom will be here soon."

"Thanks, princess." Cooper shifted his attention to Lexi and tilted his head. "Is there something else you want to tell us?"

Grace's heart raced. Lexi had confided in her, and she vaguely remembered the young girl calling her *mom* as she fell into the water. Would

Cooper accuse her of telling Lexi she was their daughter? He already blamed Grace for planning to leave and hadn't let her explain. Her pulse pounded against her skin. "I promise. I didn't say a word," she whispered.

He leaned in and squeezed her hand. "I believe you."

He did? Her eyes drifted from him to their daughter. She noticed Hannah standing in the archway.

"Mom?" His tone held an edge of reprimand.

Hannah leaned against the doorjamb with her arms crossed. "Don't look at me."

Cooper narrowed his gaze at their daughter. "Lexi?" His voice held a no-nonsense tone. Not quite scolding, but a firm, tell-me-the-truth tone.

"Fine." Lexi's dramatic sigh would have made Grace laugh if the situation wasn't so serious. "I'm sorry I spilled the secret. I should have waited. But I got scared when I saw Miss Grace go over the edge of the small cliff and into the water. It just popped out."

"How did you find out?" Cooper maintained his focus on Lexi.

The girl's shoulder lifted and dropped. "You know me and curiosity."

Cooper surprised Grace by laughing at their daughter. "Yeah, I do." Once under control, he shook his head. "Go on."

Grace studied him for a moment. The man

didn't appear to be angry. More amused than anything else. Odd. She figured he'd be upset that Lexi knew about their secret.

Lexi plopped on the floor and crossed her legs pretzel-style. "Mom left me a note in the jewelry box you gave me for my birthday."

Cooper's gaze drifted to Grace. His eyebrow arched.

"Not Miss Grace. Mom." Lexi scrunched her nose. "This is confusing." The young girl shook her head. "Mom hid an envelope beneath the velvet bottom of the box. The letter explained how much she loved me but that I had the right to know that Miss Grace was my biological mom. She explained why Miss Grace left me."

Cooper rubbed the back of his neck and took a deep breath. "I'm not sure what to say. I had no clue that your mom had decided to tell you. She must have written the letter when she found out she was dying. Of course, she expected me to give you that jewelry box on your eighteenth birthday, not when you turned eight. That was my decision. I thought it would be nice for you to have it early."

"It's okay, Dad. As you like to say, I have big ears and snoop where I'm not supposed to."

"That you do, young lady." Hannah pursed her lips, hiding a smile.

"Sorry." Lexi's head bowed. "I overheard a few conversations this week. I didn't try to. Well, maybe I did." The girl shrugged. "But after I read Mom's note, it all made sense."

"Lexi..." How did Grace explain? What should she say? She took a deep breath. "I owe you an apology."

"No, you don't. Mom explained everything. Even about your father—my grandfather. By the way, I don't like him. He's mean."

Grace swallowed past the lump taking up residence in her throat. "I have to agree with you about that. But I..." She had no words to express all the emotions crowding her mind.

"It appears Kaitlyn understood the situation better than I did." Cooper rubbed his thumb on the back of her hand.

"You were too close to see beyond the hurt." She gave him a sad smile. "You know. The forest for the trees and all that."

He nodded.

Lexi raised to her knees. A grin brightened her face. She pointed at their entwined hands. "Sooooo. Are you two getting back together?"

"Lexi," Hannah scolded.

"What?" Grace's daughter lifted her hands palms up. "I lost one mom but found another. A girl can hope, right? I mean, Dad's good at braiding my hair and painting my nails, but girl talk? I don't think so."

Cooper snorted. He turned his head and looked at Grace. "Welcome to life with Lexi."

Grace chuckled. "I can't wait." Like her daughter, she hoped Cooper wanted more than a simple friendship. But they had a lot to discuss before that possibility. Right? "You do know I intend to stick around."

"I do. I knew it earlier, too, but I let my insecurities get in the way. Something *my* mother had no problems pointing out."

The knock on the door made her jump.

"Grace, that must be your mother." Hannah strode to the front door.

Grace squeezed Cooper's hand in a death grip. She hadn't faced her mother in years, except for the unexpected hospital visit, but she didn't count that. And with the new information, she had no idea what to think about today's visit.

"It'll be okay. Mom wouldn't let Ava in the house if she didn't trust everything to work out."

"I just..." Was she ready to confront her mother? No. Not at all. But what choice did she have?

Cooper's gaze connected with hers. "If you want, I'll stay by your side."

"Yes, please." Her hands trembled at the idea of being alone with her mother, which confused her. The woman hadn't touched her or spoken to her in an abusive manner. Ava Harrison's only fault was that she hadn't protected Grace from her evil father.

Cooper shifted his attention to their daughter. "Lexi, go on out to the barn and take care of Stormy. The ranch hands are out there if you need help."

"Adult talk. Got it." Lexi bounced over and wrapped her arms around Grace's neck. "I'm glad you're my mom."

Tears filled Grace's eyes, and she melted into her child's embrace. "Me too."

Without another word, Lexi disappeared from the room, and the back door thunked shut.

"She's…" How did Grace describe the whirl-wind of a daughter?

Cooper smiled. "She's something else."

Before she could agree with him, Grace's mother stepped into the room.

Grace yanked the blanket tighter around herself as if the material would protect her from the coming conversation. Words refused to form. What did one say to a parent who stood by and didn't protect their child?

"Easy, honey. According to Izzie, she didn't know about the physical abuse. And Arthur did an emotional number on your mom as well."

Had she said her concern out loud?

"Grace." Her mother's unsure tone surprised her. "Do you mind if I come in?"

Her racing heart said yes, she cared. But that wouldn't solve any problems. *God, I'm going to need Your strength to get through this.* She was grateful that she'd begun to mend fences between her and God. He'd help her deal with the uncertainty clouding her world.

"I guess not." She gestured at the chair across from her.

Her mother sat on the edge of the cushion, her hands twisting in her lap. "I know the words are a little late, but I am truly sorry for not seeing what happened to you."

How could her mother not be aware of the cruelty her father had dispensed? "You really didn't know?"

Ava shook her head. "I heard the words, of course. The same type of words he used with me. But I had no idea that he physically hurt you."

Hurt her? Rage rose from deep within Grace. "He did more than hurt me, Mom. He almost killed me." Her voice skyrocketed.

Tears welled in Ava's eyes. "Please, believe me. I didn't know."

Her body hummed with fury. "That doesn't negate that you did nothing to stop him."

"You're right." Her mom's chin dropped to her chest. "I was afraid of what would happen if I spoke up. I should have been stronger. I should have shielded you from him."

Grace closed her eyes, processing the conversation.

"I'm here for you. I'll never let your father touch you again." Cooper whispered in her ear.

She'd longed for his love and support her entire

life. She remembered the ease with which Lexi handled the news of Grace's actions. She could learn a lesson in forgiveness from her young daughter. After three deep breaths, the buzz of her nerves eased a bit. But the years of damage lingered.

Grace thought about the question she'd wanted to ask her entire life. "Why did Dad hate me?"

Ava's shoulders drooped. "I'd like to say he didn't, but that would be a lie."

She couldn't keep the gasp from escaping.

"You see, Arthur Harrison is not your biological father."

The news hit her like a two-ton truck, stealing the air from her lungs. Was this how Lexi felt when she read Kaitlyn's letter? Thankfully, her daughter had a loving parent and not someone who abused her. "I don't understand."

Her mom's eyes drifted to meet hers. "I'm not proud of it, but I had an affair with my high school sweetheart. I hadn't intended to, but one thing led to another, and well, you know—things happened. Arthur found out, and that's when he turned mean. I don't know why. Maybe it triggered something from his past. Who knows? Then you came along, and he knew from the minute he saw you that you weren't his. His obsession with his reputation didn't allow him to acknowledge that fact in public. So, we ignored the elephant in the room, as they say."

"But why take it out on a child?" Cooper voiced the question swirling in her mind.

Ava lifted her eyes to Cooper. "Because he thought he could control Grace."

"Again, why?" he asked.

Her mother sighed. "Grace, your biological father, John, was killed in the line of duty when you were a year old. He was the sole heir of a wealthy family but loved his work as a police officer in Dallas. Arthur thought if he controlled you, he'd control your money."

That didn't make sense. "But I don't have any."

"Yes, you do."

Grace stared at Cooper and then back at her mom. "Explain that."

"When John found out about you, he wanted to be a part of your life but refused to split up my marriage to Arthur. We both knew what we'd done was wrong. I'd take you to see him a couple of times a month without Arthur knowing, of course. John set up a trust fund that only you could access when you turned thirty. However, when the time came, Arthur blocked your mail, so the letter from the attorney never reached you. You had changed your phone number, which made it easier for Arthur to keep the information from you. He'd lost his power over you and was looking for another opportunity to manipulate you into signing the money over to him." Her mother dug into her purse and removed an envelope. "I saved it for you. But I had to find a time when Arthur wasn't looking. He never left me unsupervised. When you moved out, he placed cameras all over the house. I couldn't make a move without him knowing."

The pieces of Grace's life started to fall into place. She took the letter her mother handed her and held it to her chest. She had a father she didn't know about—would never know. "I know that Arthur hurt you too. But I don't understand why you didn't report him earlier?"

"John had died. And you were a toddler. I had nowhere to go. I wasn't strong enough to leave him. Not until you served him with a restraining order did I find the courage to step forward."

Cooper stood, leaned down and kissed her forehead. "It sounds like you and your mom need time together. I'll let the two of you talk while I check on Lexi. Who knows what that girl is up to."

Grace smiled at the mention of their daughter. She wanted him to stay. To hold her while she dealt with all the secrets—all the lies—her parents had told her. But she agreed she needed time alone with her mother to unravel the past. Now that she had a glimmer into the whys of her childhood, she wanted to know more. Put the nightmares to rest. But yet, she and Cooper had so much to discuss.

"We'll talk later. I promise." Cooper tapped her nose with his finger and waltzed out.

The man really could read her thoughts. She returned her attention to her mother. With a new-found confidence, she settled into the couch cushions. She wasn't ready to forgive and forget, but she and her mother had years of pain to work through. "I think it's time we tell each other everything."

Ava gave her a sad smile. "I couldn't agree more."

The air gripped Cooper with its icy fingers. The thermometer hovered in the low forties. Not unusual for Christmastime in Texas. But since his dip in the river, the temperature felt like subzero. He raised his shoulders, tucking his ears in the collar of his coat, and burrowed into the fleece as he trudged to the barn. His stomach churned from the conversation between Grace and her mom. The truth behind Arthur and Grace's relationship disaster had shocked Cooper. The man had known no bounds for revenge—for lack of a better word—and his want for money. It had been deep and long-reaching, extending to him when he championed Grace back in the day. The rumors and untruths hurt. But nothing compared to the vile words and actions Arthur turned on his Grace.

His Grace.

She'd always been his. From the moment he met her at a young age, even with the few years' difference in age, he'd never known a connection like theirs. With her father outed in the community for his abusive ways and the killers gone for good, he planned to step up and offer Grace a future together. But first, he had to have a conversation with Lexi.

The barn door creaked open, and he stepped inside. His daughter leaned over Stormy's stall, petting her favorite friend. "Hey, princess."

Lexi jumped from the rails, ran and threw her arms around him.

He held on tight and kissed the top of her head. The secret he'd kept had to be hard on his precious girl. He'd thought he'd done the right thing, but once again, Kaitlyn had known best. Although, he suspected that she hadn't intended for their daughter to deal with the truth at eight years old. "Are you okay?"

Her head rubbed up and down against his shirt. "I'm so sorry. I shouldn't have said anything. Did I hurt Miss Grace?"

"Oh, sweetheart, no." He held her tighter.

"Mom tried to explain. I don't understand everything, but I get that Miss Grace walked away from me mostly because of her dad."

He placed his chin on her head. "That's true. And your mom and I protected Grace by not letting her know we had you." Lexi deserved the truth. Well, enough truth for an eight-year-old. "I'll admit, at first, I was angry that she didn't tell

me about you. Then your mom set me straight."
And boy, had she. That woman would stand toe-
to-toe with a rabid bear if she thought the situation warranted it.

Lexi giggled.

"When Grace met you a few days ago, she had
no idea you were her child. No one knew. Except
for your Grandma Hannah, but she never said a
word. Your mom and I wanted to respect Grace's
wishes and protect you from your grandfather."

"Do you think she likes me?" His normally
strong-willed,   let-the-world-flow-around-her
daughter's tone of uncertainty stabbed his heart.

"Oh, baby girl, I think she fell in love with you
the first day she met you here at the ranch. Before
she knew who you were."

"She's pretty awesome." Lexi smiled up at him.

"She is. She'd had a rough life, but she fought
to overcome it." Grace had changed but for the
better. No longer the timid young teen frightened
to make mistakes.

Lexi's face scrunched.

"What's wrong?"

"I don't know what to call her. Mom doesn't
seem right, but Miss Grace doesn't either."

He cupped her face in his hands. "Stick with
what you know for now. You'll figure it out as
time goes on."

"She won't be mad that I'm not calling her
mom?"

Cooper shook his head. His sweet girl always worried about others and not herself. "I think she'll be happy that you're in her life and that *you're* not mad at *her*."

He could practically see Lexi's mind spin, pondering his words. "You like Grace, don't you?"

"In a lot of ways, I don't think I ever stopped." What in the world? Having this conversation with his eight-year-old daughter was beyond weird. "I loved your mom, but Grace has always held a special place in my heart."

Lexi's nose crinkled. "I think I understand." His sassy daughter plopped her hands on her hips. "So, what are you going to do about it, Dad?"

"Yeah, Coop. What do you plan to do about it?"

He spun. Grace stood in the doorway. The light spilled in behind her, giving a halo effect around her.

A cheesy grin stretched across Lexi's face. "And I'm out." His daughter jogged from the barn toward the ranch house.

Cooper's feet refused to move. The sudden rush of uncertainty made him want to laugh. "How much did you hear?"

"Enough." Grace fiddled with the zipper on her coat, looking as uncertain as he felt.

He cleared his throat and forced his legs to work. Several long strides and he stood face to face with Grace. Her blue eyes pulled him in. But he had to know her intentions before he continued. "Do you plan to stick around?"

Without hesitation, she nodded. "Like I told you inside, I don't plan to leave you or Lexi. But I want to go back to Lackard. I don't think I can live in Rollins. Visit? Now that my father has been outed to the community, yes. Spend time on the ranch, most definitely." She bit her lower lip. "But from what I hear, you don't live far from Lackard."

"On the outskirts of town. A little bit of land. Drivable distance to work and to Stone Creek Ranch."

"Sounds perfect."

He looped his arms around her waist and tugged her close. "Perfect for us to rekindle what has always been between us." *Please, tell me you want the same.*

"What about Lexi? I refuse to do anything to hurt our daughter again." Grace scraped her bottom lip with her teeth.

The uncertainty on her face had him tightening his embrace. "I have a feeling she's all in. She likes you, Gracie. In time, she'll come to love you as much as I do."

Her eyes widened. "You love me?"

"I always have." He leaned in. Inches from her. "And I always will." He wanted to kiss her to seal the deal but didn't want to overstep. Their relationship was precarious at best.

She blew his uncertainty away and rose on her tiptoes, meeting his lips. A tentative brush at first that morphed into more.

He deepened the kiss, filling it with years of emotions. When he ended the kiss, they were both breathless.

He rested his forehead against hers, careful of the gash on her head. "Gracie, I love you."

"And I love *you*. Always have. Always will." She repeated his earlier declaration.

"Good. Because you own my heart." He rested his cheek on the top of her head.

After nine years, she was back in his arms, and he never intended to let her go.

EPILOGUE

The ten-foot Christmas tree wrapped in multicolored lights and dripping with ornaments standing in the corner of the living room had lost the mounds of presents surrounding it, and wrapping paper had thrown up all over the floor. Bows and ribbons covered the coffee table in a heap. A pile dangled precariously on the edge. One bump and the ribbons would tumble to the ground.

Kind of like Grace's emotions. One moment her cheeks hurt from smiling at the antics in the room. The next she held tears at bay at the joy surrounding her. She ran a hand over the photo album of her daughter's life that Cooper and Lexi had created and gifted to her. Her heart threatened to explode with happiness. The day had exceeded all her hopes and dreams.

The buzz of voices reminded her of a beehive as the entire Sinclair family, plus Grace's mom, sat laughing and chatting about anything and everything with Hannah. Grace's heart filled with awe as Lexi opened her last gift. A sight Grace never thought she'd experience. Cooper and Lexi had become a constant in her life over the past couple of weeks. And she couldn't be happier.

Her mom glanced over at her and smiled. The road to recovery between them had a lot of bumps, and no doubt more would come. But with her father—no, strike that—with Arthur out of the picture, Ava had changed in that short time. She'd flourished in the role of grandmother. Almost as if making up for how she'd treated Grace growing up. Grace continued to be cautious with the new relationship but encouraged her mother's interaction with Lexi. The young girl deserved the love showered upon her.

Cooper bumped her shoulder. "You look content."

"I am. I have an amazing boyfriend and an awesome daughter." She slipped her arm around him and snuggled close. "I'm sorry it took us this long to get here, but I'm glad we did." It was not the road she would've chosen, but above all, she trusted God again. Not only with herself, but with those she loved.

He placed a kiss on her hair. "We both tried to do things our own way and ignored God's path, but He brought us back to His plan. And I have no doubt this is where He wants us to be."

She nodded. During the past couple of weeks, her conversations with God had been ongoing. He was probably sick of hearing her talk. But then again, she wouldn't tire of listening to her child, so He most likely loved her nonstop chatter. Grace's cheek brushed against Cooper's shirt. "It's amazing how He can unravel our messes."

Cooper hummed in agreement.

Lexi squealed and ran over and threw her arms around her father. "Thank you, Daddy."

Grace scooted away from the hug fest and laughed at the way her daughter strangled Cooper's neck. Lexi's reaction piqued her curiosity. "What did you get?"

"A trip for the three of us to Hawaii next summer." Lexi released her dad and beamed.

Grace shifted and looked at Cooper. "Us?"

"I'd planned to talk with you before Lexi opened that particular gift." His guilty look was endearing. "Gracie, I know we still have things to work out and need more time to get to know each other again. But I don't plan on making another mistake and letting you disappear on me. I'm praying that we'll officially be a family by this summer."

A real family? She'd never had one of those. Tears brimmed on her lashes. "I think I'd like that."

Cooper brushed his lips against hers in a chaste kiss. "Good."

This. Right here, right now, was where she'd dreamed of being most of her life. Surrounded by love, laughter and a man who treasured her.

266 Christmas Rodeo Killer

Lexi wedged between them, and Grace cuddled with her daughter and the man she'd loved since her teens. She couldn't think of a better place to be than with the two people she loved more than life itself.

* * * * *

Dear Reader,

Thank you for reading *Christmas Rodeo Killer* in the new Stone Creek Ranch mini-series. Starting a new series is hard, but I'm already loving the Sinclair siblings. I hope you enjoy them too.

I'd like to send a shout-out to my awesome agent Tamela Hancock Murray and to my amazing editor Shana Asaro. You two are the best! I absolutely love working with you. And thank you to my Suspense Squad girls. Knowing there's a group of writers who I can call at any time for writing help or just to laugh is amazing. Thank you, ladies. And to my writing community, you're awesome.

Let's not forget a special thank-you to my law enforcement consultant, Detective James Williams, Sacramento Internet Crimes Against Children, who answers all my crazy questions. By the way, all mistakes are my own or are author privileges, so don't complain to him. LOL!

And thank you to my family for their love and support. Love you bunches, Darren, Matthew and Melissa!

I hope you enjoyed reading Cooper and Grace's story. If you'd like a BONUS SCENE, go to my website samiaabrams.com.

I'd love to hear from you. You can contact me

through my website where you can also sign up for my newsletter to receive exclusive subscriber news and giveaways.

Hugs,
Sami A. Abrams

Get up to 4 Free Books!

**We'll send you 2 free books from each series you try
PLUS a free Mystery Gift.**

FREE
Value Over
$25

Both the **Love Inspired®** and **Love Inspired® Suspense** series feature compelling
novels filled with inspirational romance, faith, forgiveness and hope.